Slow Fade

Rudolph Wurlitzer

SLOW
FADE

DRAG CITY
CHICAGO 2011

DC449

Drag City Web Address: www.dragcity.com

Printed in the United States of America
Library of Congress Control Number: 2001012345
ISBN: 978-1-937112-02-8 (paperback)
ISBN: 978-1-937112-01-1 (hardcover)
Cover art and design: Becca Mann

First Edition

Slow Fade Revisited

by Alex Cox

THE RETURN of *Slow Fade* is a fine thing. It's Rudy Wurlitzer's greatest work of fiction, both as a novel and as a screenplay, and one of the best American books there is. I'll get to the screenplay in a moment. *Slow Fade* the book is based on Wurlitzer's personal experiences with noted film director Sam Peckinpah, and also with the American Sixties dharma trip in India and elsewhere. Either subject would have been a fine basis for a novel. Only Rudy's restless mind could make one story of both, merging two seemingly disparate things into one mad world — one compact, entertaining, edgy, tragic, epic narrative.

One of the underlying themes of Rudy's Westerns — *Pat Garrett & Billy the Kid*, *Walker*, and the unfilmed *Zebulon* — is men who became famous heroes by dragging other, less famous men to their deaths. Pat Garrett and Billy are responsible for at least a score of killings in Rudy's screenplay: shooting deaths that were unnecessary, that could have been avoided, had the protagonists not been so vainglorious. William Walker is even more lethally heroic. The "gray-eyed man of destiny" has a body count in the thousands (not including cholera). And the relentless Captain pursues Zebulon, the mountain man, no matter how great the collateral damage.

So *Slow Fade*'s Wesley Hardin drives his family to its doom. Unable to direct pictures, the old director decides to direct people and events instead, and a fragile, messed-up family situation takes on new dimensions of demented drama. Wesley Hardin's complex family wasn't Peckinpah's; it is Rudy's invention, and the two men's careers are notably different. Hardin has directed thirty or forty films in many genres and made a substantial fortune. Peckinpah made a dozen features and lived in a trailer. Yet the character of Hardin is utterly, entirely Peckinpah. Wracked by all manner of ailments and addicted to cocaine, alcohol, and controlling others, Peckinpah was the greatest director of Westerns since John Ford: a contradictory, brilliantly talented, sometimes terrifying man. Rudy wrote *Pat Garrett* for Monte Hellman to direct, but the studio gave it to Peckinpah, the Western guy, instead. He gutted the script, turning it from a lonesome, existential tale whose heroes didn't meet until the very end into a story of old buddies who betray each other's code. The screenwriter didn't necessarily appreciate the process, but what the director was doing was transforming Wurlitzer's script into a Peckinpah film. Almost all Peckinpah's films, and all his Westerns, were about old friends betraying each other's code, and by God, *Pat Garrett & Billy the Kid* would be, too.

The chapter where Wesley, fired up by a silver bullet full of coke, decides to shoot an unscheduled scene involving Pancho Villa in the middle of the night, knowing it will get him fired and the film shut down, which it does, is a vintage Peckinpah moment. Yet Rudy combines all of this very specific Western madness with something which one might naively associate with serenity: the "mystic East." His own trajectory had taken him on travels such as these, and so, just as he drew Wesley from life, he writes about the crowded, hectic, disorderly, incoherent world of the dharma bums with some authority. That world, too, of young Americans and Europeans seeking to find spiritual authenticity or just get away from their parents was one Rudy once inhabited, or transited.

Slow Fade is not a long book, and it is a pleasure to read, but it is by no means "light." It moves, inexorably, from continent to continent, like a 747, low on fuel, whose undercarriage won't come down. Disaster looms. And the one character who, if there were any justice, should pay the penalty for this wrecked, calamitous set of circumstances, doesn't. Wesley Harding just keeps on tickin'. Like Rudy's Western heroes, he is built of devilishly epic stuff.

Walker, Wesley's son, provides the story-within-the-story of *Slow Fade*, a narrative of what has happened to his missing sister, Clementine, written for his perverse father in the form of a screenplay. Rudy wrote the book in 1982–3, I think. It was first published in 1984. It has such great characters and scenes that several directors encouraged him to write a screenplay based on it. (I was one of those directors.) He wrote the *Walker* screenplay in 1986, and we shot that film in Nicaragua in 1987. So I'd guess Rudy wrote *Slow Fade*, the screenplay, in 1988.

We wrote some other scripts during that period, together and apart. One was about the trade in infant body parts, and one about the contra war, but none of them, and nothing else, came close to Rudy's screenplay based on the novel *Slow Fade*. It is one of the best scripts I have ever read, incredibly disciplined in all its choices. The characters it cut, the locations and scenes lost from the book—all its choices were the right ones.

For starters, Rudy took the pages Walker wrote for his father and made them the set-up. The character of A.D. disappeared, becoming incorporated into Walker (as the screenplay son was now known) and giving him more of a desperado quality. Jim became Walker again, luckily. The annoying cameraman Sidney became an even more obnoxious limey documentary producer who wants to make Wesley's life into a reality TV show. Prescient or what? In the screenplay of *Slow Fade*, the action moves from Beverly Hills to Monument Valley (where Wesley's last Western is being filmed) to India. It is mesmeric and seamless, and it retains the book's most marvelous scene, where the young travelers are snake-poisoned and robbed aboard their luxury train compartment. The biggest surprise of the screenplay, for those who have experienced the book, is the self-involved director's decision not to go to Labrador, but to follow his wife and children to India. This provokes a cataclysm, like all acts of well-intentioned colonialism. And in India, beside twin funeral pyres, the screenplay ends.

Rudy and I worked with a top producer, Lorenzo O'Brien, to try and get *Slow Fade* the movie on. But the obstacles overwhelmed us. The script was a downer, it was set in India, and characters got killed. (Movie stars don't like to die.) No one would make a film with the commies who made *Walker*. One day Rudy ran into a Thai prince and, like a master chef, whipped up a *Slow Fade* set in Thailand. But the Indian version was the killer, the one we all three wanted to exhaust ourselves on and lose our shirts on once again. The script was that good.

The film of *Slow Fade* has yet to be made. As Joe Strummer observed, the future is not yet written. In the meantime, here's the original, with a broader canvas than the script, more characters, and more locations, written when the old scribbler was just getting into his stride.

"You're A.D., right? The doctor or shrink who's taking care of Walker."

Sure I am.... And now it's time to meet the prototypical, disposable, identity-shifting Wurlitzer hero: musician, road manager, doctor, Hollywood producer, screenwriter, Mr. A.D. Ballou.

Alex Cox
Southern Oregon
April 2, 2011

Slow Fade

THE PHONE woke him.

"A.D.," the voice said. "What twisted little cul-de-sac do I find you in now? It took my secretary an entire week to track you down."

"Uptown someplace. I don't know. Should I know?"

It was Arthur somebody. New-age impresario. Record producer. Asshole.

"Are you open for business?" Arthur asked. "I need a road manager."

A.D. sat up and lit a cigarette. Fuck Arthur somebody. The room looked like it had been shaken down by a junkie. Everything was on the floor, including a two-foot cactus. The girl next to him rolled over on her side, moaning softly in her wretched dreams. He no longer loved her and she no longer loved him. All that had been decided the night before.

"I need you in Santa Fe for two weeks," Arthur was saying. "A grand a week plus expenses."

A.D. was already reaching for his traveling shoes.

"Santa who?"

"Fe. The road manager split. The group is Gang Greene. Melissa Greene's attempt at a comeback. She's lost her pipes and half her cerebellum as well, but a gig is a gig. Right?"

"Right. Fifteen hundred and I'm your man."

"Call it twelve," Arthur said and hung up.

He called his ex-wife and told her he was paying her five hundred of the three grand he owed her. He didn't make any other calls, not even the necessary ones. He didn't wake the girl and he didn't write a note. All of that was understood. He just colored himself gone and flew out to Albuquerque, New Mexico.

In Albuquerque, A.D. rented a Chevy Malibu and drove up to Santa Fe, purple clouds drifting across the evening sky like giant bones. Halfway there he pulled over to the side of the road, inhaling the vast sweet desert. He felt light-headed and goofy although he wasn't on anything but the intoxication of being snatched out of New York at just the right time. Over the long dirty haul A.D. was an escape artist, not a prime-time player, and he was ready to pull the plug on New York. He had come there six months ago from Miami for a record gig that never happened and he had never found his stroke. He was always half on the street, half in somebody else's set of descriptions, his days a sullen list of distractions that kept him slightly stoned, hustling the minimum number of gigs to get by, writing a few songs for a few people, never testing his solitude or the courage of any one action. So a roll toward the West was a welcome roll, especially if it ended in L.A. He knew how to survive in L.A. His rhythm felt better, and he could always find work as a studio musician or drift into some semi-hard hustle on the edge of the entertainment world, shooting location stills, best friend to a declining star, shiatsu foot massages for Beverly Hills matrons. If all else failed there was always dealing dope or flying back to New

York, honing in on his old action like a mutated animal trying to rediscover a genetic pattern. All of which made him a coast-to-coast man. Except for those miles in between, which he now had to think about.

A.D. always bought his wardrobe on the road, believing that it gave him an edge to wrap himself in something new. In Santa Fe he bought a pair of blue and white Tony Lama boots, a black Levi jacket, and a gray Stetson. He was a large fleshy man in his early forties with an unkempt red beard and pale unfocused blue eyes, and the new threads, rather than cushioning a generally wasted appearance, only made him seem more sinister. Which he liked, he decided, checking himself out in a full-length mirror before he went down to the Fried Adobe on the outside of town.

The Fried Adobe stood between a Taco Burger stand and a Texaco station. Inside, a tired country and western trio sang "Moon over Tulsa" to a table of drunken college kids and two silver-haired businessmen arguing over their bill. After a brandy and soda at the bar, A.D. went back to the dressing rooms. Gang Greene were all there and they weren't waiting for him.

Melissa Greene lay on a badly sprung couch, her eyes hidden behind dark glasses. Her long legs were wrapped in tight leather pants, her broad shoulders and sagging breasts in a green silk shirt. Her braided hair had been dyed green and her fingers, wrists, and neck were covered with green jewelry. The three members of the band sat around a table, drinking Wild Turkey from a bottle and dipping slabs of roast beef and ham into a large jar of mayonnaise. They all wore green suits with thin green ties and green basketball sneakers. Their dyed green hair was cropped short, all except for an emaciated black man whose oblong head was completely bald.

"I'm the new roadie," A.D. said.

No one answered or acknowledged him, an attitude that A.D. accepted and even welcomed.

He sat down at the table and lit a cigarette. After he had smoked half the cigarette, he asked what time the set went on.

"No time," the black man said. He stood up and looked down at Melissa Greene, his eyes full of malignant confusion. "There ain't going to be no set. No nothing. Nowhere."

Melissa swung her long legs over the edge of the couch and took off her glasses. Her eyes were flat and glazed.

"You have a contract, Charlie," she said, looking at the floor.

"I got a contract with myself, baby," Charlie said. "And that's the name of the game and that's it."

Melissa stood up. Through the layers of makeup she looked old and stretched and burned out.

"Then get the fuck out," she screamed. "You've been sandbagging me from the beginning."

"You've been sandbagging yourself, not that you got that much to sandbag. You're a psychotic wreck, sugar. I mean that sincerely."

Melissa picked up the jar of mayonnaise and turned it over, a large glob falling on Charlie's shoulder.

He stood there letting her do it.

"You always wanted to be an albino," said the drummer, a thin-lipped man with empty blue eyes. "Green never did suit you."

The other member of Gang Greene picked up his guitar.

"That cuts it," he said and left the room.

Charlie watched him go, then ripped Melissa's silk shirt from her body. He slowly wiped off the mayonnaise before he walked out the door.

The drummer wrapped up the roast beef and ham in a napkin.

"For the road," he said and followed Charlie.

Melissa went back to the couch and sat down. A small elegant tattoo of a red dagger pointed down between her breasts. She looked at A.D.

"Fuck me," she said.

"I don't think that would be appropriate."

"What's appropriate?"

"I won't be able to get it up."

"You'll never know unless you try." She sighed, her impulse over. A.D. asked if he would get paid.

"No," she said. "Everyone's on their own from here on out."

He offered her his jacket, which she absently accepted.

"You can drive me back to the house for my things," she said. "I'm clearing out."

Melissa drove. She told A.D. the story of her life but he didn't listen, having too much trouble with his own story. She turned off the main highway and followed a dirt driveway ten miles to its end. Two station wagons and a VW van were parked in front of a broken-down pickup truck. To one side stood a barn and a corral hosting three horses. Beyond the corral lay the shimmering moon-lit desert.

"We've been staying here like some fucking commune," Melissa said. "It's the club owner's hobby ranch. The whole thing is a night-mare."

He followed her around the side of the house where she turned to face him on a brick veranda framed with earthen jars of cactus and portulaca.

"They think I killed the other piano player. Owen."

"I pass no judgment," A.D. said. "I just want to get to L.A."

Melissa sat down on a white wicker couch. Leaning back against a pillow, she shut her eyes.

"I suppose in some way I helped Owen do himself in," she went on. "In those vicious little ways we all contribute to the general death of a relationship. Can you catch the song in that?"

"Probably," A.D. admitted. "The melody anyway."

"Now that my career has gone down the toilet, I'm going to pack and drive to L.A. Why don't you help me open the new chapter of my life? I'll pay for your car and your gas and your motels, and you'll help me drive and explore my needs, which are considerable."

He accepted but called for a slight delay.

"I'll take a ride on one of those horses over there and then sleep until I wake up. If you're still around I'll drive you to L.A."

He took his Levi jacket off her shoulders because the night had turned cold and because he wanted to stiff her a little. Then he walked over to the corral and saddled up a bay mare.

Swinging up into the saddle, he walked the horse toward the desert, the first hint of dawn giving definition to high clumps of gray sage. A.D.'s father had owned race horses at one point in his short, checkered career, and that had been a time they had shared together, driving out to the track outside of Cleveland in the early morning. But the horses weren't fast and his father wasn't either, and after he was caught bouncing bad checks from Ohio to Iowa, he skipped bail and was never heard from again. He must have had moments like this, A.D. thought, at the mercy of whatever weirdness was coming down the road. It depressed him thinking about his father and how lame he was. His own head felt separate from the rest of his body, as if out of control somewhere on its swivel. He needed to drop anchor, not let a nameless horse carry him over country he felt no connection to. As if to answer this sudden need for a direction, he guided the horse down the banks of an arroyo, but the arroyo came suddenly to an end and he had to hold on to the pommel as the horse scrambled up onto the desert again.

He rode on, prodding the horse into a loping stride, his mood changing as the sun pushed over the horizon like a squashed tomato. He was shaking loose a bit, riding into open space, and fuck the rest. The acrid smell of the sage enveloped him, his mind slacking off as he rode into a dense forest of piñon and juniper. A twisted branch whipped against him, drawing blood across his forehead. But A.D. was so deep into the mythology of his ride that he accepted the pain as initiation, and riding back into the open again, he permitted the glory of the day to elevate him once more. The horse tested the reins, wanting to stretch out, and he let himself go the rest of the way as well, flat out if that was meant to be, and they galloped across the desert and then down along the banks of a stilled green river.

A rifle shot broke the thunder of his ride. Then another.

Heading straight toward him along the banks of the river galloped two runaway horses and their riders. It was an apparition that was never to leave A.D., one that he would visualize constantly, without warning, always in slow motion, the figures swaying toward him as if under water.

As A.D.'s horse bucked up a steep hill, the first rider passed him, her long black hair flying out behind her as she hung grimly on to the horse's mane, a look of amazed terror on her face.

The second horse swerved up the hill, galloping neck and neck beside him, its rider rising high in the air over the saddle, his elongated arms and legs flopping about in total abandon. He managed to let out a yell and looked toward A.D., a sly smile on his pale emaciated face, as if some part of him was watching over the whole mad plunging ride, even as his body flew over the horse's neck toward the ground.

A.D.'s horse swerved again and ran straight back across the desert. More shots rang out followed by a line of horsemen appearing over the crest of a hill. It dimly occurred to him that they were Indians and that they were preparing to let fly a volley of arrows in his direction.

A.D. saw the arrow quite clearly as it fell out of the brilliant blue sky and felt the unwavering surge of his horse riding forward to meet it. Then there was total blackness followed by oblivion.

He woke later—they were to tell him two days later—conscious only that his head was wrapped in bandages and that he was alive. When he woke again the darkness and pain remained. His hands traced the bandages over his eyes and the thought of being blind made him fade out once more, curling in on himself, whimpering and moaning like a small animal.

Still later, he woke once more, screaming out.

A hand lightly touched his wrist.

"You've lost an eye," a man's voice said. "Your other eye will be all right except that it's traumatized and you won't be able to see out of it for a few weeks. It's a kind of localized hysteria."

"Which eye is gone?"

"The left."

"Are you the doctor?" A.D. asked.

"Unfortunately, no. But I read your chart. I'm the last person you saw before you rode into that arrow. I'm Walker Hardin."

As if on instant replay, he saw again that mad puppetlike figure flying over the horse's neck.

"You crazy asshole," A.D. said. "You almost killed me."

"It's true." Walker's voice was soft and matter-of-fact. "You came close to dying."

The hand removed itself from A.D.'s wrist and he could hear Walker pouring a glass of water.

"My horse spooked," Walker explained. "And then Evelyn's horse lost control. It was a spectacular ride."

"Fuck you and your horse and your spectacular ride," A.D. said. "What about the Indians?"

"They were Apaches about to scalp three mountain men."

The image enraged A.D. "There aren't any mountain men in the desert," he yelled.

"They were on their way to Mexico to get laid."

His hand reached up to his blind eye. He didn't care about any of this bullshit. One entire eye had been eliminated from his head and he wanted it back. He didn't want a black patch or some piece of round glass. He wanted the cocksucker's eye and he reached out for Walker. An eye for an eye.

Walker took hold of A.D.'s clawing hand and lowered it down by his side. His grip was like a handcuff. "We all rode onto a movie set," he said. "You spoiled the first shot of the day."

"You mean none of this is real?" A.D. asked.

"The arrow must have been real."

"The arrow?"

"Yes. The arrow."

"Well, I'm going to sue somebody," A.D. said. "Half my vision is gone and somebody has to pay for that."

"How much do you think half your vision is worth?"

"Worth? How do I know what an eye is worth? I won't have any peripheral vision or depth of field. That's a definite handicap."

Walker didn't answer. A.D. thought he would ask for two million dollars to start with and then come down to a million, bottom line. The idea of losing an eye and gaining a sack of gold seemed like the deal of a lifetime.

"You might have a hard time collecting from the movie people," Walker said, as if he had been lurking outside A.D.'s mind. "Their lawyers are all on retainers and they have nothing to do but slow things up and fuck around with you. They also found some drugs in your pocket which they turned over to the sheriff."

A.D.'s hopes slid to the bottom as fast as they had streaked to the top.

"As fate would have it, my father is the director of this miserable film," Walker said. "He'll certainly try and make a deal with you because making deals is how he goes about things. If I were you I would certainly listen to what he has to offer."

A.D. could hear Walker slowly and painfully shift around in his chair.

"Are you badly smashed up?" he asked.

"A broken shoulder and a few cracked ribs. Nothing that won't heal."

"Who was the girl?" A.D. wanted to know. He was starting to drift off, but he didn't want Walker to leave without knowing who the girl was.

"My father's wife" was the answer.

"I'm freaked," A.D. said.

"What of?" Walker asked, his voice gentle and sad, coming from far away.

"That I won't make a deal," A.D. whispered.

"What kind of a deal?"

"Any kind. A deal is a deal. I just want to keep moving the furniture around. I don't want to be caught at home practicing scales."

He wasn't making any sense. He wanted to say more about the deal and hear what Walker had to say, but words wouldn't form and then it was too late and he was rolling back into painful sleep.

Walker remained next to A.D. while he slept, watching over him with somber gaze, listening to his shallow, constricted breathing. A pack of Marlboros lay on the night table. Using one hand because of his neck and shoulder wrap-around cast, he slowly opened the box and tapped out a cigarette. Lighting a match, he held the flame up to the cigarette in his mouth and inhaled deeply. He hadn't smoked in five years, or perhaps it was longer, and the smoke made him dizzy and immediately caused his lungs to ache. But he had needed the violation somehow and he was glad as well for the steady pain in his shoulder, as if that raw focus might help him to review the past few chaotic days, even up to the obscure and perilous present.

When his plane had landed at the L.A. airport a week ago after a seventeen-hour flight from Hong Kong, there had been about fifty minutes when Walker hadn't known where or who he was. When the other passengers stood up to leave the plane, he stood up as well even though he had no idea where the line was going or even if there was a line. He moved forward because everyone else was moving forward, his mind seized with such sudden paralysis that only his body seemed capable of an act and then only if there was no need for a decision or a known direction. On the outside he looked odd as well, his tall, emaciated frame covered with a lemon-yellow Taiwanese silk suit three sizes too small for him, black alligator shoes with no socks, and a wild confusion of blond hair falling to his shoulders. The customs official asked him three times to step forward and when he finally made the commitment it took Walker another few minutes to realize he had left the carry-on canvas bag containing his passport back on the plane. Another official, silver-haired and obviously of a higher rank, asked Walker please to follow him to a side room.

As Walker entered the room, a short muscular man in mauve slacks and blue Lacoste tennis shirt offered him his hand.

"Roger Woods," he said. "Your father's attorney. You'll be out of here in no time."

"No time," Walker said with a sigh and sat down on a chair. "But that's the way I've been traveling. At least lately, that is."

Both the attorney and customs official took a closer look at Walker's pale green eyes, but his disorientation was so extreme that it was impossible to tell if he was stoned or just one of the crazies that show up on Pan Am flights from the East. In any case, drugs or a mystical loss of faculties wasn't the issue. Walker's canvas bag appeared and was placed on a table. The silver-haired official spread out the contents with the objective detachment of a surgeon: white cotton pants, dirty underwear and socks, a Hindi-English dictionary, a John D. MacDonald paperback, a small clay statue of what looked to be a Buddha with a red hat on, a torn notebook, a faded Polaroid of Walker and a dazzling blond girl in a sarong standing arm in arm in front of the Grand Hotel in Calcutta, and finally the passport. The official thumbed through it with one hand, reading off the stamped litany:

"India for quite some time I see, Nepal, Thailand twice, no, three times, South Korea, Japan, Hong Kong. You are well traveled, Mr. Hardin."

"Well traveled, yes," Walker agreed.

"You were out of this country for two years and you've let your passport lapse for over a year. That is quite a serious oversight on your part. In different circumstances you would be in serious trouble."

"Unfortunately there are only these circumstances," Walker said, as if they were in the middle of a serious discussion. "At least there are no other circumstances that I am aware of in this way, I mean."

The official scrutinized Walker to see if he was being a wise ass, but it was obvious from the way Walker was staring at one of the attorney's blue Topsider sneakers that his mind was way off to the side of any kind of attitude.

"Let's just say for the sake of brevity that your father has a friend in a very high place," the official said.

"The President," Walker said matter-of-factly.

The room was silent, no one having wished that awesome title to be actually expressed.

"Well, Wes Hardin and the President have certainly spent personal time together," the attorney said, nodding to the official as he picked up Walker's bag and gently guided him out of the room and down the long corridor to the baggage claim area.

As they stood waiting for the bags, the familiar smell of ozone and car exhaust penetrated through the protective envelope that Walker had wrapped so firmly around himself. Staring outside the glass door at the passengers drifting through the smoky congested light, he began to recognize with every organ of his body, if not his stunned brain, the airless aura of the city, his city, and it was then that he finally let himself know that he was home.

"You'll fly out to Santa Fe tomorrow," the attorney said. "The production secretary will drive you to your father's home for the night. If you'll give me your ticket, I'll get the rest of your bags."

"I have no bags," Walker said.

"No bags," the attorney repeated, as if that was information he couldn't deal with.

Walker followed the attorney as he pushed through the door into the slow flat air and walked over to a black BMW. The attorney opened the door and threw the canvas bag into the backseat, waiting for Walker to climb in. Shutting the door behind Walker, he reached down through the open window and squeezed his shoulder. "It's damned good that you came home. It will make a difference to your father. He's not in the best of shape."

The BMW pulled away from the curb into the flow of traffic heading for the San Diego Freeway, and for the first time Walker noticed the driver. She wore dark glasses over a thin sensual face and her black hair was pulled behind her into a bun. A professional, Walker thought. Like Lauren Bacall in *The Big Sleep*, although Lauren Bacall hadn't really been professional or was he thinking of another movie? It had been a long time since he had thought of a movie at all but whoever she was like, she was certainly calm and contained, not saying anything or even looking at him.

She drove past the freeway and turned north on La Brea. It was evening and there was a line of office buildings that hadn't been there two years before reaching up into the smog and the dark shadows of the Hollywood Hills. He was almost sure they weren't going toward his father's house in Beverly Hills, and making a great effort that caused a slight stammer, he asked if his father had moved.

"He still lives on Mulholland," she said in a soft nonprofessional voice. "He wanted me to take you up to the Griffith Observatory before going home. He said that you might be spaced-out or disassociated or something and would need some time. He gave me a list of instructions for your reentry."

"I'm sure he did," Walker said.

The Griffith Observatory was where they had shot *Rebel Without a Cause*, a handle his father had often used on him and an association Walker was sure his father had been aware of when he dictated his list of reentry instructions. He became suddenly panicked when he couldn't remember James Dean's companion in the film.

"Do you remember who the kid was in *Rebel Without a Cause* with James Dean? He died at the end."

"Sal Mineo. They called him Plato. He was killed a while ago. In real life, that is. Some kind of fag drug scene."

They turned up the steep road to the observatory and pulled into the parking lot. Beneath them millions of lights shone through the gathering darkness like electric night flowers. Walker got out of the car and walked over to a bench. He felt slightly faint and sat for a while just concentrating on his diaphragm moving up and down. He had forgotten about the girl when she put her hands lightly on top of his head. It was a gesture that he was not prepared for and his thighs and arms began to tremble.

"Why were you away so long?" she asked. "I didn't even hear about you until a month ago."

"I don't know, really. After a while it was too hard to get back."

"I always wanted to do that," she said, sighing. "Just take off and fuckola movieola."

As her hands dropped to his shoulders, he shut his eyes. Surely she wasn't doing what she seemed to be doing, her hands now rubbing against the back of his neck.

"Are all of these moves on the reentry list?" he asked.

"So far, yes."

"If they weren't, would you do this anyway?"

"If I wasn't riding for the brand, I wouldn't be here, if that's what you mean."

And then it was too late as she dropped to her knees in front of the bench, her cheek rubbing against his protruding cock. He wanted with all his heart and soul to withdraw, to let his member defiantly wilt under her caress, a caress that was now involving her thumb and forefinger as she unzipped his fly. But it had been more than a year since he had had an erection much less an orgasm, and heart and soul were not enough to stop the throbbing swell within him. Oh, fuck his father, he thought, that he would have conceived of this scheme, this little hired bitch in front of him, kneeling under his distant direction, her mouth now wet and immense as it circled around him for the arranged Welcome Home, Son. A spurt was now beginning from his toes, shuddering up his trunk, and causing him nearly to lose consciousness as he came and came down to the last squeezed drop. Afterwards she drove him in silence back to his father's house on Mulholland, a professional to the end and, as she nodded good night to him from the car, not without tenderness.

A Mexican maid whom he didn't recognize answered the door of the rambling Spanish Tudor house with its view of the San Fernando Valley which he avoided looking at as he followed her into the *entrada* and down the inlaid Provençal-tiled steps to the massive oak-beamed living room with its stone fireplace and Japanese and Eskimo artifacts hanging on the wall. It was clearly not the room for him to be in, and rather than accept the drink the maid was offering him he said he would prefer to go to his room. She informed him impassively that his room, the room that he had been raised in and always slept in when he visited was "*no más,*" the "*señora*" having taken it for herself. He followed the maid out a side door and around the side of the pool to a guest cottage he had never seen before.

The two-room suite, with kitchenette and sauna, was clean and white with freshly cut roses on the dresser in a blue china vase. He sat down on the king-sized bed but immediately rose, feeling an overwhelming need to touch or smell something familiar. He stepped outside to the pool, a body of water he had no trouble remembering. But as he sat down on a deck chair, he discovered that even that familiar space had been rearranged.

"Hi there," spoke a robust English voice from the far side of the pool.

Walker dimly made out a man's head protruding from a bubbling Jacuzzi. The Jacuzzi, too, was new, as well as another guest cottage behind the end of the pool.

"Just landing?" the man asked. "I detest that flight from New York, although the one over the pole from London is a thousand times more horrific."

"I came in from Hong Kong," Walker said, trying to remember if they knew each other.

"Whatever." The man's head disappeared and reemerged like an inquisitive seal. "But I don't envy you that project. Detroit in the summer is not my cup of tea, although I seriously doubt if the old bastard will ever get to it."

"What's wrong with him?" Walker asked, sure now that he had been mistaken for somebody else.

"I suppose he's just run out of whatever primitive fuel his motor requires; rage, fear—who knows? But don't misunderstand, I'll definitely shed a tear, perhaps two, if he drops dead and not just because it'll cost me more than a few quid if he doesn't finish this current shoot. As it is, he's three million over with all the usual demented nonsense going on.... But I love him like a brother, or perhaps a half-brother."

Walker got up and went into the house. No one was around and he walked upstairs and entered his father's room. It hadn't changed in over thirty years: piles of scripts on his mahogany desk, the overflowing floor-to-ceiling bookcase, the huge bed framed with elephant tusks, the two Modigliani nudes and the map of Venice on the wall, his hand-tooled guns resting in their Chippendale glass case. The only evidence of the new *señora* was a floppy straw hat on the seat of a wicker armchair.

He walked down the hall and entered his own room. Everything had changed. Gone were the original drawings of the sets of three Busby Berkeley films his father had given him on his thirteenth birthday; the framed picture of his now dead mother standing next to her Cessna, looking like Amelia Earhart in a flying outfit, his father peering dimly out of the cockpit; and his books and all the rest of the list he was incapable of recalling. They were all gone. Replaced by bare white walls, an austere single bed, a simple desk made from oak planks, two straight-backed unpainted wooden chairs, an old captain's chest, and a round hand-stitched rug. He picked up a photograph on the desk showing a small girl of eight or nine, a puppy in her arms, standing in front of a man and woman, all of them dressed in woolen pants, heavy boots, and parkas. The man's Indian face, severe and unsmiling, stared straight at the camera, while the woman, pale and white-haired, gazed at the top of her daughter's head with a wistful smile. Behind them smoke drifted out of a tar-paper shack, a mountainous pile of wood off to one side.

He walked next door to his sister's room. It, too, had been stripped of its past and made into a library-TV room. All except for her books, which were still in their wall-to-ceiling bookcases, and one framed photograph over the new white couch. He studied the photograph as if looking for clues. His sister, blond and pale and fragile, stood next to him on a tennis court. They wore immaculate white shorts and T-shirts, holding their racquets out to the side as if ready to receive a volley from across the net. They were both smiling — his sister less so, but she had always been more reluctant when it came to games and social activities. He must have been sixteen and she, of course, two years younger. There was nothing in her face to suggest any inner turbulence, nothing more than a pretty Beverly Hills teenager smiling for the camera.

Walker lay down on the couch and closed his eyes, immediately falling into an exhausted sleep.

The next morning he missed his plane to Santa Fe even though the maid woke him and the driver waited outside in the limousine. Taking a later flight gave him time to have the maid cut his hair and pick out some clothes for him on Rodeo Drive while he remained in bed. When he finally landed in Santa Fe his appearance had changed considerably. Although still gaunt and ravaged, he looked, at first sight, like a mannequin in a store window, with his new

Adidas sneakers, French jeans, and brightly checkered sport shirt.

The film's publicity director drove him west into the desert through a crimson evening streaked with purple flares. It was dark when they reached the set, a collection of trailers and trucks parked off to the side of a dirt road winding down near a small river. His father would be shooting all night and was busy at the moment with his first setup. Walker waited in his trailer, pouring himself a large shot of tequila and watching television for the first time in two years. An hour later his father arrived, a tall, wiry man with a white beard and blue, red-rimmed eyes.

At first Wesley Hardin didn't see his son lying in the rear of the trailer watching TV without the sound, involved as he was in a heated discussion with the producer.

"I don't care who the fuck he is," Wesley was saying, turning to face the producer as the man came in the door after him. "He won't see the rest of the rushes until I'm ready to show them and he won't pull the plug. He's in too deep."

"You didn't hear him this morning on the phone. I did. He was screaming. The whole studio knew about you urinating on the screen at dailies last night. It will be in the trades tomorrow."

"The camera was out of focus for the fourth straight day. I had to fire my focus puller and my operator, two men I've worked with for ten years."

"You're five million over, Wesley," the producer said evenly. "No one cares about excuses when you're five million over."

"Is that why you're flying to L.A. tonight to sabotage me?"

"I'm keeping the studio off your back, which necessarily involves not telling you everything."

"That must be why you didn't tell me about the memo you sent them yesterday on my age, drinking habits, and all-around perversity."

"You are an obnoxious man," the producer yelled suddenly. "An unholy cocksucker of the first rank."

The producer's impulsive attack was unexpected and left Wesley's lower lip quivering with rage. As he reached for the tequila bottle, he saw Walker watching him from the rear of the trailer.

"Betrayal, cowardice, deceit," he muttered, breaking the bottle over the edge of the kitchenette's Formica counter and advancing toward the producer, who quickly retreated out the door.

As Wesley turned to face his son, Walker was struck by the collapse in his father's once taut face, how the entire head seemed to hang by an invisible hinge, as if even the weight of gravity was enough to make it sag forward. Otherwise, Wesley Hardin looked the same as he always did, for he never changed his outfit on location: faded jeans, a white shirt, hand-tooled cowboy boots, and a fold-up Panama hat.

"You look terrible," his father said, advancing toward him and letting the tequila bottle drop to the floor.

"You don't seem in top shape yourself," Walker said, tentatively meeting his awkward embrace and smelling the brittle decay and booze on his father's skin and the cool shadow of something more.

"Are they going to can you?" Walker asked, reaching for something to say.

"They probably should although they don't have the balls. But the whole rotten project is out of control."

They sat awkwardly facing each other over the trailer's kitchen table, Wesley opening up another bottle of tequila and pouring them both drinks.

"You could have come back once or twice," Wesley said, his mouth twisting into an odd little grin. "That's a line I had this kid say to Wayne once, in *Bitter Creek*. You remember? The kid was so nervous to have a line with the Duke he couldn't say it without stammering, and I had to fire him."

"'I came back,'" Walker said. "That's more than I thought I'd ever do. That's what the Duke said. I was an extra on that one."

Wesley sighed, his hand shaking underneath the table. "I thought you'd be here a few days ago," he said abruptly.

"I arrived in L.A. last night. One of your production assistants met me."

"How was the welcome home party?"

"I didn't appreciate it."

Wesley poured himself another shot of tequila and downed it before he forced himself to look directly at Walker. "Do you have any news about your sister?"

"No. Not really. Not past a certain point."

"What do you mean, point? What point?"

"The point where you don't know what anything means any more and it's every man for himself. I don't know. I never saw her over there. I heard plenty about her. But so did you. You read that detective's report, didn't you?"

"What else did you hear?" Wesley asked warily.

"Various things." He looked away from his father, not able to pursue it any more. "There are people around who might know what happened. I might be able to get to one of them."

Wesley's tone was raw and impatient. "When?"

"When I get to one of them. Certainly not before."

"Will you?"

"Will I what?"

"Get to one of them?"

"If I get around to it. I guess so."

"You *guess* so? That's not good enough."

"Good enough?" Walker asked, feeling a curtain come down between them with terrifying swiftness. "What do you know about good enough?"

There was a knock on the door followed by the assistant director's blond head.

"We're ready to roll, Boss, any time you are."

Wesley rose, relieved to be summoned. "Hang around, or I'll see you at the hotel tomorrow for lunch. We're shooting all night and we'll probably try to get a magic-hour shot. They're after me like a pack of wolves so I won't have much time. But we'll talk on the ride back or something. We go to Mexico in a few days for three weeks, and the whole business should be finished in less than two months."

"I don't have any plans," Walker said.

"That's what I'm afraid of. Do you have money?"

"Your lawyer gave me a few grand in L.A."

Wesley paused as he went out the door. "I'm married again. You might like this one. She's from Labrador. Her grandfather knew your grandfather."

Walker went back to the rear of the trailer and lay down, falling immediately asleep. He woke before dawn. The trailer was empty and he stepped outside into the cool night air keeping away from the dazzling arc lights and fog machines and walking toward the area that had been staked off for the horses.

A thin woman in tan corduroy pants and red flannel shirt was saddling a horse, one of the wranglers looking on. She moved with relaxed assurance, tightening up the cinch and swinging her long frame into the saddle. Her long black hair hung behind her in two knotted braids, and as she turned her face Walker knew that she was his father's new wife. She had the same level look to her blue eyes as the girl in the photograph.

"You're Walker," she said, gazing down on him. "I'm Evelyn. Do you want to take a ride?"

He nodded. She looked no older than he, somewhere in her early thirties, with the broad cheekbones of the Inuit as well as the blue eyes and thin nose of the Scotch. His father had married a breed. He must have finally gone home and that's where he must have met her.

The wrangler brought him a saddled horse and he rode after her as she trotted down the dirt road and out along the banks of a slowly moving river. She urged her horse into a gallop as the sun broke over the horizon and it was in trying to keep up with her that Walker lost control, his horse running flat out across the desert until the collision with A.D.

AND THAT was what Walker recalled, not exactly in that narrative form, of course, but in that general sequence, until finally, toward dawn, A.D. woke again.

"I'm here," A.D. said. "Who's there?"

"Walker."

"Don't fuck with me, Walker. Because of you being such an asshole, I'm pinned here with no eyes, no gig, and not too much hope."

"What would give you hope?"

"A deal."

"You'll get a deal."

"Is there some kind of watch on me?" A.D. asked, suddenly nervous that Walker was just sitting there staring at him. "Am I in worse shape than they've told me?"

"You're the same," Walker said. "I'm just sitting here wondering if you have any pain pills."

"I take all they give me."

"How many years have you been on the road?" Walker asked.

"Too many. I've been through it all on the road."

They were silent and once again Walker watched an obscure night give way to an equally obscure dawn.

"Did anyone from the band ask for me?" A.D. asked.

"The nurse told me someone came by to say they had checked out."

"Who are you, anyway?" A.D. asked. "Aside from being your father's off-the-curb son."

A.D. was experiencing an almost overwhelming wave of fury, an emotion which, while it expressed itself, made Walker feel strangely relieved.

"I've been on the road myself, one way or the other," Walker replied, "and I probably know less than you about what comes next."

"Does that mean there's no deal?" A.D. asked.

"Something might be arranged," Walker said. "To fit our needs. One way or the other."

Having approached that decision, he eased himself out of his chair and slowly shuffled out of the room.

LATER that day, Wesley Hardin and his wife, Evelyn, arrived at the door of Walker's hospital room. Evelyn opened the door, gasping at the way Walker's head tilted to one side, one arm hanging over the bed. There was such intense suffering in his face, as if his open mouth had crystallized into a silent scream, that she waited until she saw him breathe before she shut the door.

"He's asleep," she whispered.

"We'll try the other guy," Wesley said.

They moved down the hall and entered A.D.'s room.

"A.D. Ballou?" Wesley asked. "I'm Wesley Hardin and next to me is my wife, Evelyn, who was riding with my son when your horse got away from you. We're all concerned about your accident."

"If I was you I'd be concerned, too," A.D. said. "I'm asking for full compensation. I was attached to my left eye, more even, than my right, being as how I'm left-handed."

"I can understand your feelings and, hell, I sympathize with you," Wesley said. "But unfortunately you're not in a great position to ask for damages. You rode past two clearly marked No Trespassing signs and avoided the signals of a guard stationed at the edge of the mesa. Not only that, but a substantial amount of nose candy was found in your jacket pocket, a charge which we have, for the moment, been able to have suspended. Despite all this, however, we are, in good faith, willing to cover your hospital bill as well as your travel expenses back to wherever it is you want to go."

"Good faith doesn't play with me," A.D. said.

Wesley pulled up a chair near the head of the bed and leaned forward. He was tired and his day had been bad and he didn't want to be there.

"Look here, Mr. Ballou," he said with an equal mixture of intimacy and weariness, "I'm putting it to you straight. We have to work this out now or not at all. Making a film is like being on a fast train. Once off you can hardly ever get back on again. I'm flying to Mexico tonight never to return to this little candy-assed town."

"Now is okay with me," said A.D., who was having trouble listening.

"Good," Wesley said. "I talked to Walker on the phone today. He's sleeping, which is just as well because what I want to say concerns the two of us as much as it does him. He says you've written songs and other stuff as well, including screenplays."

A.D. realized the ball had been thrown to him, that Walker had somehow set something up, and he did the only thing he could to keep the ball in play: he lied.

"I've written a few," he said, inventing himself on the spot. "My uncle wrote screenplays. We did *The Big Deal* together."

"Whatever," Wesley said, staying very much on his fast train. "I know that you and Walker have talked and that you've found common ground together and common ground is a precious thing when you're standing on quicksand."

"Amen," A.D. said.

Wesley stood up and walked over to the window, trying to form an idea, or perhaps it was a hook, in any case something to wrap around A.D. and maneuver him into whatever angle he might come up with. Wesley was a master at impromptu story conference, being well known in the industry for turning almost certain defeats into spectacular commitments from the money people, but as he turned to face the bed he found himself not so much making a pitch to A.D. as awkwardly revealing Walker's back story.

"Two or three years ago, God, I don't even remember exactly, but Walker had just gotten married and his sister, Clementine, had gone off to India to study the sitar or some such instrument. When no one heard from her for six months Walker and his wife decided to go over there and look for her. I was working and ending a rotten marriage and not paying much attention to him or anyone else, including Clementine. Although I did make a few high-level calls, one to the Canadian prime minister and the other to a senator, and they both said they would put professionals on the case. It relieved me and I didn't think any more about it. I was even pleased she was off on an adventure and had made some kind of a break from L.A...."

He walked over to Evelyn, standing beside her and nervously twisting his fingers into the thick strands of her black hair.

"I guess in those days Walker was a little confused. He was drifting around, trying to promote an all-girl rock-'n'-roll band and developing a few scripts. I had given him a job as assistant producer on a film and when he consistently failed to show up I had to fire him...."

"You don't have to get into this right now," Evelyn said.

"I want to get into it right now," Wesley insisted. "Did you know that his wife died over there?"

"I didn't know."

"I found out this morning. From his doctor."

"Listen," A.D. said, having managed to grasp only the bare drift of Wesley's tale. "All I know is that I'm blind in one eye on account of one of your Indians and I want to get paid off for the loss. It's that simple."

"I encourage you to sue the pricks," Wesley said, not breaking stride, even relieved to be forced away from the story. "Not only that, but I will give you the name of a lawyer who is an expert on such matters. But of course it'll take more than a few years to see any money at all—that is, if you're lucky, which I surely hope you are."

Wesley left his wife's side and went back to the chair near the bed, pulling it up to A.D. and leaning forward toward his ear. He breathed deeply for a few minutes, as if summoning up enough energy to think through the deal.

"What's on my mind now, A.D., is what you're going to do while you're waiting to get back into shape."

"I'll go along with that," A.D. said. "What am I going to do while I'm waiting to get back into shape?"

"I owe you a period of recuperation," Wesley said. "It being my wife, my son, and my Indians that caused you to lose your eye. With that in mind, I arranged a house for you and Walker outside of town. I want you to consider writing a screenplay with Walker that somehow includes his recent experiences. I'll give each of you ten grand up front, twenty more on delivery. "

"What are you talking about, something to do with pages, or what?"

"It doesn't matter. I never pay too much attention to the actual script. If you want to use a cassette, that's okay."

"In other words," A.D. said, making a stab for the bottom line, "you want me to make a connection with your son, file his story on what happened to . . . it's your daughter, right? . . . and if a script happens, so much the better, it's all a write-off anyway."

"I want to make an investment in communication," Wesley said, trying to smile at Evelyn despite lines of fatigue appearing like sudden squalls at the corners of his mouth and eyes. "Mine, yours, Walker's . . . Evelyn's. I don't have much time. I only have a few cartridges left in my chamber and I have to make each shot count."

"It'll cost you extra." A.D. made one last effort to advance himself. "I'm not used to crossing from one medium to another."

"Ten grand more for the script, to be divided between you and Walker, and another five for your services as companion and witness."

Wesley stood up and kissed Evelyn on top of the head. "I'm late for a meeting but I expect to hear from you soon, A.D."

"One more thing," A.D. said, his mind beginning to drift. "Is this all bullshit or are you going to do this film?"

"Absolutely I am going to do this film. I can find private financing for a film in India. Renoir did one. Malle was over there. Even Rossellini did one."

"I thought it was all bullshit," A.D. said.

As Wesley left the room, A.D. reached out vaguely for Evelyn, for someone, and to his surprise he found his hand being allowed inside the warmth of hers. Falling asleep, he muttered an old Muddy Waters song: "'I got a black bone, I got mojo too. I got John the conqueror root, I'm gonna mess with you. I'm gonna make you girls lead me by the hand. Then the world will know I'm the Hoochie Coochie Man.'"

Evelyn sat holding A.D.'s hand until he fell asleep. Then she went down the hall to Walker's room. He was awake and looked up at her from the bed with distant eyes.

"That was a good ride," she said, sitting down on the edge of the bed. "I'm sorry it ended badly for you."

"My horse spooked," he said. "And then I spooked."

"Your father wanted to see you before he left but you were asleep. He'll call from Mexico."

"Mexico?"

"You didn't know? He'll shoot there for four weeks. In Durango. We leave tomorrow morning."

They were silent while a nurse came in and gave him a pill. Evelyn sat not altogether contained in a black cotton shirt that hung loosely over her firm breasts, a simple necklace of bleached bone around her neck. When the nurse left the room she spoke again.

"Your father said just now that you and A.D. Ballou are going to write a screenplay for him to shoot in India."

"How much is he going to pay?"

"Ten thousand, I think. Is it that important?"

"It's a large consideration," Walker said. "I mean, considering what he's really asking for, what it really means. But don't worry about India. No one in Hollywood is going to bankroll Wesley Hardin in India."

"He says the film will happen."

"He says everything will happen short of salvation, but in his black heart he only counts on ten percent."

"He thinks he's dying," Evelyn said softly, looking at him directly so that Walker knew what she said was true. "The doctors can't find anything wrong with him, but he's losing weight and he just seems to be letting go of everything. I thought directing this Western would help because he hasn't worked in over five years. But it hasn't helped. It's only made it worse."

"It's temporary," Walker said, not prepared to accept the information and trying to fend off this recurring echo that no one anywhere had any time left. "He's fallen apart before. It's part of his myth that he can always rescue himself and everyone else around him."

"I know," she said absently.

"You met him in Labrador?" Walker asked.

"He was on a location trip."

She walked unsteadily over to the window, raising it a crack and letting in a small shiver of air.

"I guess you can't just tell him directly all you know about Clementine and be done with it?" she asked.

Walker didn't answer and Evelyn sat down on the edge of the bed and then lay down on the floor. "I'm tired," she said from the floor. "And a little stoned and I'm not used to being stoned. I'm used to being drunk. At least lately."

Walker, from where he lay on the hospital bed, couldn't see her and for a moment he even forgot she was there, until she spoke again:

"He'll try and avoid whatever he has to avoid and then it might be too late. But I guess you know about that."

"Yes," Walker agreed. "I know about that. It runs in the family."

"He doesn't have much peace. I never thought he did, even when I first met him. But that's what I needed then. I mean, the opposite of peace. As a way of cutting loose. I don't know. I don't know about any of it now, to tell you the truth."

"I don't either," Walker said, only catching the end of what she was saying.

"But you set up the deal on India as much as Wesley did," she went on as if talking to herself. "Well, that's between you. I don't know if it concerns me. I could ride out of here right now. I could get on a bus and go anywhere. But I wouldn't go north. I don't think I'd do that."

Walker let himself fall asleep with a sudden rush. When he awoke later that afternoon, Evelyn was gone, which is what he had wished for when he closed his eyes.

THREE DAYS later Walker and a subdued A.D., wearing a black eye patch, left the hospital, and were driven northwest toward the Utah border by one Caleb Handy, an ancient ex-stuntman and now rancher who had been on most of Wesley Hardin's films from the early thirties up to the present. A.D. had not been given official permission to leave the hospital. His good eye had not come around yet, and he was pinned to the dark rhythm of his ride on four Percodans, nodding in and out of Caleb's long-winded raps as they all three sat in the cab of his three-quarter-ton AMC truck.

"Now, son, listen here," Caleb was saying to Walker, squeezed in the middle. "Your daddy had an edge on him in those days. Don't think he didn't. He could slice the bullshit out of an actor and not even be on the set, that's how hard he was. It was the ambition in him that gave him the juice for that kind of good hate that moves people off the dime. In those days he believed his mother lode would never dry up and he'd always be able to tap his source. Now he's strip-mined himself, the same old moves and hand-me-down situations, the good stuff going into making a deal, but look here, son, I ain't one to complain. I don't give a damn what the show is, I never look at 'em and to tell the truth I don't believe old Wes does either...."

Walker let him ramble on, drinking from the bottle of Wild Turkey they passed back and forth and staring out at the purple line of melancholy buttes, dust and red sand swirling around the truck from an approaching storm. They left the pavement and went straight across a sandstone mesa, brush and juniper on either side of the road, the A.C. turned all the way up to protect them from the fierce dry heat. As they climbed upward the desert gave way to scrub oak and stands of yellow pine. Even A.D. seemed to smell the growing sweetness in the air, yawning and snorting through his wretched dreams. Caleb shifted into four-wheel drive, the truck growling through a washout and over a narrower, rougher road. A hawk circled above them and a deer peered out from a clump of dogbane. Inching over a steep rise, they came upon a deep green meadow framed with straight stands of Douglas fir. A stream snaked its way across the meadow and hunches of cattle grazed on the tall dewy grass sprinkled with blue larkspur. On the far side of the meadow a large ramshackle house made from thick cedar logs stood on a slight knoll looking out across the mountain toward the southwest. To one side stood a barn, a bunkhouse, and several corrals.

A large-boned gray-haired woman in a faded campaign jacket and loose-fitting khaki pants came around the side of the house, shading her eyes from the slant of the evening sun.

"You boys look to have enjoyed yourselves," she said as Walker and A.D. staggered out of the truck. She looked at Walker, shaking her head. "You must be Wes Hardin's lost and found son. Last I set eyes on you was that ski film up in Idaho."

She helped A.D. inside the house and into a bedroom off the high-beamed living room while Caleb led Walker into an adjoining room.

A.D. slept through the night and the next day and when he woke again the house was silent around him. Sitting up, he thought his eye distinguished a shade of darkness, and swinging his legs over the edge of the bed, he fumbled for the light. It was true, vague forms swam before him. He rose from the bed and made his way toward where he thought the door should be. It was there, and gaining confidence he stepped into the other room, realizing he was no longer in the hospital. He crouched on all fours and tried to crawl back to where he had come from, but the wall met his advance and he sat back, trying to regain his composure.

A growling form hurled itself against him, knocking him over. He cried out, swinging blindly, but the dog, rather than closing his fangs around him, licked his body with a rough tongue. He stood up and felt his way around the room, past a stone fireplace, a floor lamp, and a table and chairs, the dog padding alongside him. Finally he found the piano. He sank heavily onto the stool as if before a refuge and his long ringed fingers stretched out lightly over the keys and he came alive again. "Just an old road man," he improvised, finding a few simple chords. "One eye lost / one deal made / not knowin' the cost / what's been played...." He played the beginnings of a few old tunes, but mostly he was content to sit there.

"Jesus, I thought you were Caleb." Walker stood at the side of the piano looking down at A.D.'s naked figure hunched over the keyboard, at the pale gray skin that had never experienced direct sunlight.

"Your daddy pay us any coin yet?" A.D. asked.

"A grand each, the rest to come as we have pages."

"Well, this is your hustle," A.D. said. "You set up the deal with your daddy so you must know what he wants."

"I suppose," Walker said.

"And India is the hook," A.D. went on.

They stood and sat together in silence while A.D.'s fingers

stroked the piano keys. Then Walker helped A.D. to his room and then went to bed, listening to the night sounds outside and wondering if he would or even could find a form to tell what he had to tell or if the form had somehow found him.

In the days that followed Walker took short walks to the edge of the meadow and beyond, sitting in the cool depths of a spruce forest or following a winding brook as it descended the mountain through groves of quaking aspen and willow trees. Mostly he kept to himself, Caleb having gone to Denver to buy a horse and A.D. content to play the piano, sometimes singing with Amelia, Caleb's wife, who would stand beside him, a bottle of Johnny Walker on the back of the piano, belting out blues and old ballads in a high hoarse voice. A.D. and Walker encountered each other only at the evening meal, an event that Amelia produced with enthusiasm, baking breads and pies and putting on the table an enormous spread of vegetables and freshly butchered meat. Walker avoided the meat, but his entire body seemed to respond to everything else, and almost immediately he began to put on weight.

One day Walker came upon a clearing on the southern face of the mountain. Sitting on a slab of granite under a hard blue sky, he gazed out over the distance and for a moment experienced calm and even joy before such a desolate and remote horizon. But his mood was eclipsed by overwhelming rage, a thick choking bile rising within at the thought of his father and the deal struck between them. Let him die in his own way, he thought, in his own time. And it was at that moment of absolute refusal that Walker did, in fact, give in to his father, an image of his sister appearing before him as he had come to imagine and invent her, standing in the clear piercing light of Namche Bazaar, the snow peaks of the Mahalangur Range behind her, a patched purple shawl over her thin shoulders, her round head shaved to a bristle, her dirt-encrusted hands methodically moving over a string of prayer beads.

That evening Walker went to his room and didn't come out for three days. Refusing all food and drinking steadily from Caleb's stash of Johnny Walker, he lay in bed and watched TV while listening to the radio, from the earliest soap to the late, late show. Sometimes he watched with the sound off, other times with the radio on or the image off and the sound on. On the afternoon of the fourth day, A.D. entered Walker's room. Walker was lying on the bed in his Jockey shorts watching a game show.

"Are you dead or alive or what?" A.D. asked.

"I want to move around for a while."

"We don't have any pages so we don't have any bread so we can't move around."

"You're right," Walker agreed.

A.D. sighed. "I could help grease it along and we could take it easy and build up a stake and then go our own ways, but if you can't get to it . . ."

"I appreciate your lack of hope," Walker said and he meant it. "But I've thought about the story and we can probably shovel enough pages together to get a first payment and then we'll buy a van."

"A van?"

"There's someone I want to see in Albany."

"Well, there's someone I want to see in L.A., more than one, in fact. Like my lawyer."

"As you pointed out," Walker said, "it's my story so it's got to be my drift."

"Whatever," A.D. said, wondering how long it would be possible to ride on this particular track.

Walker handed him a bottle of Johnny Walker and turned the sound down on the TV, leaving on the image. Then he lay back and shut his eyes. A.D. turned on the tape recorder that Wesley had given him and the tape was almost halfway through before Walker managed to begin.

WE CUT FROM BLACK... *to a husband and wife, she in their king-sized bed, he in his pajama bottoms walking around. Agitated. No. Scratch that. Move it forward. They're in this same elegant room, their bags are packed and they're about to leave. They're in their early thirties, healthy, a little straight, she more than he perhaps but she's a real knockout, blond, uptight, but strangely erotic. We'll call them Jim and Lacey and they've been married for five years and Jim works for his father in the auto industry where he's a vice-president. It's old money, Grosse Pointe money, and that's where they are now, in the bedroom of their summer house on Lake Michigan, one of three houses on Jim's father's estate, the other two houses belonging to his father and sister, we'll call her by my own sister's name, Clementine, for a natural hook.... There's tension in their bedroom as there has been for several months and once more Lacey almost desperately pleads that she doesn't want to go searching for some weird sister-in-law who went off to India to study the sitar and who hasn't been heard from in eight months. She doesn't need that kind of a trip. She needs to find something to* do, *a job, an identity, something for herself. Jim is wired and impatient and says angrily that if she doesn't come with him it will end their marriage, that they no longer communicate with each other and that they need an adventure like this to hold them together; not only that, but his father, Pete, or Pistol Pete Rankin as he's known in the industry for his quick moves with women and failing corporations, is very likely dying and has every right to want to see his daughter again, not to mention the fact that Clementine might be in some kind of terrible trouble. Lacey closes her eyes and says, almost in tears, that he is a manipulating control freak who will stop at nothing to get his way, not even emotional blackmail. Jim, very tight-lipped and vicious, tells her that she is a cold withholding cunt.... She slaps him and he holds her wrists, forcing her to the floor. "Yes, I'll go," she says through clenched teeth as he looms over her, causing her pain. "You prick, you fucking bastard, yes," as he begins to make love and she opens up to him, wanting him, hating him, "yes, oh yes"...and so on as we...*

CUT TO FATHER AND SON... *with Jim walking toward the family boathouse across a manicured lawn like a putting green while Pete Rankin is rowed to shore from his forty-eight-foot sloop. Stepping carefully onto the dock, P.R., as he is also known, is a prototype Captain of Industry: white-haired, barrel-chested, cold blue eyes, patrician nose; and yet on second glance there is something frail about him, frightened even, his voice hesitant, his eyes unfocused, distant.... They walk into the boathouse where Pete pours them a drink from a pitcher of already mixed martinis waiting in the well-appointed bar....*

THE INTERIOR *of the boathouse reflects as much if not more of the family tradition, at least from the male side of the lineage, than does the baronial nineteenth-century manor house that can be seen through a window, high on a hill overlooking the lake. Two single racing sculls lie neatly in their racks, oars crisscrossed above them. Handcrafted oak furniture, massive and imperial, stands before the stone fireplace, pictures of old Yale rowing teams over the mantel..."I talked to the Indian ambassador by phone a few hours ago," Pete begins. "He still says that they haven't been able to turn anything up, that there isn't all that much one can do when someone disappears over there."... "I still want to go," Jim says.... "It's foolish," his father says. "We've hired top men. Professionals, and they'll have a better chance of finding her than you or any other amateur."... "I don't think so."... "How can you, in all conscience, say that?" The father is on the edge of anger but cannot, will not allow himself that emotion.... "Because I know her," Jim says.... "At least wait until the board meeting, a month more won't make that much of a difference. I need you here if we're going to keep control of the firm."... "She might need me there if she needs to keep control of her life."... "Romantic rubbish," the father says stiffly. "She's probably off having an affair with someone and the mail got delayed. She's never been known for keeping in touch."... "I hope you're right but I'm still going to go."... "And you're taking Lacey?"... "She's my wife. She goes where I go." The father pushes his son to the precipice. "When you come back you'll have to face a few decisions."... Then without a word, he leaves the boathouse and Jim watches him through the window as he walks up the long hill to the main house... and then we* CUT TO INDIA....

THAT WAS the first installment that was read, first by Evelyn as she sat by the empty pool of the Hotel Ambassador in Durango, Mexico, then later that night by her again, reading the pages to Wesley as he lay face down on the bed of their suite in a blue silk robe, a cold towel over the back of his head.

"At least he didn't make them from Boston or New York," Wesley said, having listened to most of it.

Evelyn placed the pages on the bedside table and stretched out next to him. She was almost the same height and she was naked except for a black T-shirt with *Mountain Gold* stenciled across the chest in gold letters. Raising one slender yet muscled leg in a right angle to the bed she let it slowly come to rest over the back of his thigh, noticing through the silk robe how shrunken and hollow his buttocks had become. She still desired him sometimes although they rarely made love, and when they did it was nearly always the same: lying on his back, his head propped up by a pillow, he would watch her as she slowly seduced his tired cock into arousal. Often he would be soft at first and she would hold him with both hands, licking and sucking and placing him up between her strong pointed breasts and as he grew hard she would rise up and settle over him, letting him slowly enter into her, making an offering of control as she waited, barely moving, until he swelled even and she could begin to move. Rather than reach out for her own pleasure, she would curl back toward him and fold into herself as he softly directed her, whispering and touching her and finally having her lean away from him so that he could watch her ass and because he loved her dark broad back and the strength in her neck and shoulders and it was sometimes then that he remembered why he had married her.

Only now there was no response from underneath the towel or silk robe.

"I don't think it's too bad," she said. "Sloppy and weird because it's so intense, but it seems like a story."

"It isn't good or bad. It isn't anything."

She could feel a coiled tension leaking out of him, like the red message light on the phone that had been blinking on and off for the past hour, and she moved off the bed and slipped into a pair of white slacks and shirt.

"You started it, didn't you?" she asked. "I mean with that strange man, A.D. Ballou. Pulling him into a project with Walker."

"I didn't start it," he said abruptly. "It came oozing up like the snout of some swamp animal. I simply lassoed the opportunity."

"I don't understand why you're drawn to him, to people like A.D. Ballou."

"Because he still believes in change, no matter what the price. It's the American way, in case you haven't noticed. Besides, Walker needs a connection to that kind of malignant hustle to get back on his feet, to find the courage to tell me his tale. The boy is off his feed, and I don't want him looking to me for nourishment. That way we'd both go hungry."

"Maybe that's true about Walker. I wouldn't know what he needs. But didn't you believe in change when you married me?"

"Not really. I was more attracted to your romantic belief that you could change through me. I found it touching and painfully nostalgic. It made me want to protect you, to expose you to change but not the illusion of it."

"And now?"

"Now you're looking to change again. At my expense. For protecting you too well."

He stood up and, letting the towel drop to the floor, went into the sitting room.

He didn't recognize the two men sitting stiffly on the couch. One wore a mottled array of buckskin and furs, an otter cap pulled over the top of his gaunt face, a long jagged scar across his cheek. The other man was older, with a twisted white beard and baggy pants held up by rope suspenders.

"You asked to see us about a wardrobe check," the older man said.

"What scene?" Wesley asked.

"In the saloon where we ask Pancho Villa if he'll hire us as mercenaries."

"What happens?" Wesley asked, pouring himself a shot of tequila.

"Pancho Villa shoots Hank," Scarface said. "After we tell him our credentials and ask where we can get laid."

"Why does Hank get shot?"

"Pancho Villa tells me that I've lost my courage," Hank said. "He says that I'm too old and cynical to be of any use and he just pulls out his pistol and shoots me."

Wesley took the script from the older man and looked at the pages where his lines were underlined in red. He tore out the pages and handed the script back.

"I think we'll just go out to the set and shoot the fucking thing," he said.

"You mean shoot the scene now?" Hank said.

"Right now. On the set," Wesley said and walked into the bedroom.

"I want to get it over with," he said to Evelyn.

"Get what over with?" she asked, thinking that he meant get himself over with.

"The film. The whole thing. Are you ready to hit the road?"

"Where to?"

"Who cares where to," he said angrily. "Are you ready to hit the road?"

"Wesley, ever since I've known you we've been on the road."

"Well, do you want to get off the road?"

"Yes. I would like to get off the road."

"Good."

He called the second unit cameraman and told him to meet him on the set with a 16mm camera and the sound man. Then he called the Mexican actor playing Pancho Villa and told him they were shooting the saloon scene and to be out there as well.

"But it is ten o'clock, Señor Hardin," the actor said, his speech slowed by a combination of booze, Quaaludes, and sex.

"Bring her along, too," Wesley said and hung up.

He pulled on whatever was closest—red sweat pants, maroon loafers, Hawaiian shirt.

"*Por los bandidos,*" he said, slipping a .38 revolver into his belt.

In the hotel lobby Wesley came across a few more actors and some of the crew and told them to hire taxis out to the set and the studio would pick up the tab. He said that if they wanted to bring anyone else out that would be okay too. Then he called the production manager and told him he was going to shoot a scene and to round up the usual suspects. The production manager said that Wesley was going too far, that he couldn't cover for him in any way if he pulled a stunt like that. Chalmers had flown down from the studio three hours before and was already kicking everyone's ass and he wanted a meeting with Wesley at 8:30 a.m. tomorrow to discuss the very real possibility that Wesley might not be in sufficient command of himself to go on and that they were fully prepared to send another director down and even had one picked out. Wesley said that he was open to discussing everything, that he felt in firm control, and that he was even considering the production manager as a possible coproducer for his next film which was going to take place in India and in view of the difficulties involved would really be more of a producer's picture than a director's.

In the El Presidente bar, Wesley and Evelyn had three quick shots of tequila with the prop man, who was sitting with an aspiring actress from Mexico City making ends meet, so to speak, as a paid weekend companion. He asked the prop man, an old-timer and a millionaire from all he had stolen from Wesley's films, to meet him on the set with a case of booze and anything else that would encourage altered states of behavior. The prop man said with tears in his eyes that he would pull out all the props as this might be the last scene the "old man" would ever be allowed to shoot. Just to prove or to underline his gratitude and loyalty he pressed a silver bullet full of pharmaceutical cocaine into Wesley's palm and kissed him on the lips.

On the street Wesley interrupted a four-man mariachi band serenading a Greyhound bus full of German tourists, offering them each one hundred dollars American to come out to the set and play.

"Say no more, *jefe*," said the trumpet player. "We are yours forever."

Then Wesley and Evelyn and the two actors who had been in his suite for a wardrobe check drove north twenty miles to the set, a collection of nineteenth-century houses and false fronts lining both sides of a dusty main street complete with saloon, hotel, and jail. A few Mexican families lived in and maintained the town, moving from house to house as each movie company came through and tore apart and rebuilt everything according to the dictates of their script or the inclinations of the director.

A single streetlight was on when they drove up in front of the saloon, the guard waving a tired salute toward Wesley as he stepped out of the car.

"*Por la revolución,*" Wesley said, handing the guard a bottle of tequila and striding past him.

The saloon was half complete, being in the middle of a transformation from the lobby of a Mexico City whorehouse to a border town cantina with crude wooden tables, low smoke-blackened ceiling, and a bar where several jars held live tarantulas and the curled form of a diamondback rattlesnake. Wesley took a table at the far end, facing the swinging doors. Pouring half the pharmaceutical coke on the table, he fashioned six rough lines, snorting them up with a rolled peso note and handing the note to Evelyn.

"You are my life," he whispered, kissing her on the ear.

"Is that why you are trying to end it?"

"Not end, precisely, to come to terms with, to slowly dissolve, perhaps."

"Why not just cut to black," she said, inhaling the rest of the coke.

"Why not, indeed."

He peered at the two mountain men who had taken up positions at the end of the bar. "Good boys," he said. "Solid boys who can hit the mark."

"You intimidate me when you're like this," she said.

"I've never been like this," he said, looking past her as the swinging doors opened and five of the crew came in, standing awkwardly just inside the door. The sound man walked over to find out what was going on.

"I'm going to try for another point of view," Wesley said. "A Nagra would be best because I might want to drift around the room with the sixteen. If you can't go small, then set up the best you can."

"Is this a test?" the cameraman asked, sullen about the whole thing.

"It's not a test," Wesley said sharply, the sudden rush from the cocaine, a substance he rarely used, making him raw and impatient.

"And it's not a rehearsal. I just want to take a quick slant away from the story for a while. If that's okay with you?"

"I don't care one way or the other," the sound man said and walked away.

"I'm going to get someone to drive me back to the hotel," Evelyn said.

"Stay. *Please*," he implored her, motioning to a grip standing nearby.

"Set up a minimal amount of light," he told the grip, swinging his attention back to Evelyn: "I want you to be in this."

"In what?"

"This footage. Tonight."

"Why?"

"Why? Do I have to know why? Because I need you to be here."

She nodded, retreating into the refuge of her own silence, a gesture that in the first days of their relationship Wesley had been drawn to, even obsessed by, as if he had recognized in her sudden withdrawals the raw stoicism of his own family, the internal solitudes of that dark land he had run so far from and lately had felt such a pull toward. Only now he felt Evelyn's silence as an abrupt refusal to comment or participate on any level and he took it as a rejection.

The prop man entered, followed by two Mexicans carrying a case of liquor and bags of potato chips and fried chicken. Behind them trailed three local whores dressed in brightly flowered print dresses, snapping their fingers and trying to get stoned or drunk as quickly as possible. Everything was flat and stale and awkward.

Wesley stood up and walked over to meet the second unit cameraman coming into the saloon with the mariachi band.

"Are you set up?" Wesley asked.

"I can shoot right now," the cameraman said, setting down an equipment case and taking out a 16mm camera.

"I don't want you to think about the script," Wesley said.

"I would prefer that," the cameraman said. He was young and

unhealthy and obnoxiously alert, moving around in his safari jacket as if on a combat mission.

"Pan across the bar to my wife sitting at that back table," Wesley directed. "Then move with me up to the table as I sit down, give me a brief two shot, and then it's all on her, no matter what she says."

As they moved toward the table, the mariachi band broke into "La Cama de Piedra" and one of the whores in a loud abrasive voice translated the lines to the prop man: "I have a stone bed and a stone pillow. The muchacho who lives with me has to be true...."

Evelyn watched them come, despair clouding her dark eyes.

"I don't like this, Wesley," she said as he slid into a chair beside her.

"What don't you like?" he asked.

She looked at him, her eyes suddenly flat and hard, wanting to hurt him for the first time. "I don't like your fear. I don't mind your rage but I don't like your fear. It makes me despise you."

"What do you think about this film?" he asked.

"I think this film is pathetic and I think the way you're trying to do yourself in is bullshit."

The camera held on her as she walked away, through the door and into the street, and then panned back with the drunken arrival of one of the Mexican drivers dressed as Pancho Villa as he walked up to Wesley to find out what was going on.

EVELYN walked down the street, the sad trumpet from the maria-chi band following her as she went through the false front of a bank and out onto an open field. She realized that she was very drunk and sat down at the end of the field on a pile of flat rocks. In front of her a patch of light spilled over the littered yard of an adobe house. She must have dozed off, for she was startled by a hand pulling on her shirt. A small girl, naked and solemn, stared at her with round black eyes. Evelyn made no effort to speak or smile and just sat on the pile of rocks. A trickle of urine ran down between the girl's legs. Behind her an old woman appeared in the doorway of the house, her thin Indian frame covered with a gray Civil War jacket several sizes too big for her. The girl ran back inside the house and Evelyn looked directly into the woman's ancient eyes. The old woman said something in Spanish, giving a slight almost imperceptible shrug toward the house, and Evelyn followed her inside.

A large room was divided by a wall of canvas stretched across a clothesline. Two men sat at a table playing dominoes. One she recognized as a local wrangler who also doubled as one of Pancho Villa's men, a role he had no trouble qualifying for with his full black mustache and heavy-lidded eyes. The other man, wearing a Boston Red Sox jacket and a battered gray Stetson set low over a thin copper-colored face, was one of the stuntmen that Wesley had brought down from L.A.

The old woman sat down on a double bed in the corner, next to a plump woman in a Japanese housecoat nursing a baby and watching a game show on TV which she never took her eyes from.

"*Indio*," the old woman said, pointing to Evelyn standing in the doorway.

The wrangler pushed out a chair from the table for her to sit on. "She thinks you're Indian."

"I'm half Eskimo."

The wrangler explained that to the old woman in Spanish, who fired back a reply, which he translated: "She says there's thousands of Mexican Indians playing baseball in the States so why shouldn't some of your Indians come down here and play?"

The wrangler poured Evelyn a shot of bourbon from a half-empty bottle on the table, which she drank quickly. The room was warm with a thin layer of smoke underneath the ceiling from a leaky open fireplace, and there was the smell of dogs and cooking oil and baby urine that made her feel connected to another room at another time.

"Wes is shooting a scene," she said, wanting to say something to blunt the force of this unwanted nostalgia. "Pancho Villa in the saloon."

The wrangler stood up. "No one told me they were shooting Pancho Villa in the saloon."

"No one told anyone anything," Evelyn said. "It's a free-for-all scene and it doesn't matter."

"I have two lines in that scene," the wrangler said. "'I don't mind killing him' and 'To hell with the revolution. Let's go for the gold.'"

Evelyn watched him put on his hat and go, knowing that she should leave with him.

The stuntman looked at her with cold black eyes. "At least Wes is going out with his boots on."

"I guess," she said.

The stuntman poured himself another drink, then filled her glass as well. "I'll tell you one thing, Mrs. Hardin. There's no way in hell I'm going over and watch the old bastard pull the plug on himself."

"I know what you mean," Evelyn said, watching the stuntman pour himself another drink. He seemed slightly crazy but somehow in control.

"Of course I'd sign on for him again even though he fired me day before last. You understand he likes to fire me. Fired me one time in North Dakota and once in Hong Kong. I get a load on and bust up something or somebody and he fires me. But he takes me back. I think he has a weakness for half-breeds."

"I'm a breed," Evelyn said. "And I think he has a weakness for me, but I don't know if I want to go back."

"Oh, hell, of course you're going back," he said impatiently. "You can't leave a man like Wes Hardin when he's down."

"It seems as good a time as any," Evelyn said, wondering if she meant it.

"You're Canadian?" he asked.

She nodded.

"I suppose you married him to get out of town. Hell, I don't blame you. I know what Canada is like. I broke a foot up in Calgary in a car stunt."

"It wasn't like that."

"See it through anyway. Who cares where anyone is from or what it was like? I'm part French and Moroccan and it's never done a damn thing for me."

His face was flushed from the booze and confessions of mixed blood, and Evelyn found him violently handsome. He sat there pouting, his lower lip feminine and full, his eyes staring past her, focused on some inner turbulence. She knew she was getting sloppy, but it was as if she had to run her own parallel course to Wesley's, to step across her own boundaries while he was breaking up his.

"In some secret way I know you more than I know Wes," she lied.

"Because we're both breeds?"

"Because neither of us makes plans and Wes has to have a plan or he'll die."

"Maybe that's why he's so shaky. He's run out of plans."

"Maybe."

"He has more fear than we do. You can smell it on him."

"You have fear and I can smell it on you."

He looked at her with great care. "What am I afraid of?"

"Of me, for one thing," she said softly, smiling at him.

He didn't answer. Behind him, the woman in the Japanese housecoat changed channels.

"I'm not afraid of you," he said finally. "I'm afraid of Wes."

"Maybe it's time you broke that one."

She stood up, dizzy from the booze and the smoke and the dull knowledge that she had gone too far with him.

"I'm going for a ride," she said. "I love my husband."

"I don't know about love," he said, wanting to hurt her.

She leaned on the table looking down at him and then abruptly left.

He stood up as though drugged and followed her out the door where she stumbled over a twisted pile of bailing wire.

Reaching out to steady her, his hand brushed across her breast. She gasped, leaning against him, and it was then that he knew just what it was she wanted done with her.

They walked silently across the field and down the back end of the street, past the false plywood fronts of the town. Suddenly she was unable to go on. Shouts and trumpet blast washed over them from the saloon and then receded. They were standing next to the jail in the shadows of an overhead balcony. She let him pull her to him, his mouth finding hers in a surprisingly gentle and tentative kiss and then she abruptly turned and walked into the jail.

The ground floor was full of lighting equipment and she picked her way through piles of cables and generators and up a narrow flight of stairs to the second floor, his footsteps following behind. Moonlight fell through a barred window outlining a sheriff's office with a rolltop desk and a rifle case. Two cells, their doors open, occupied the rear. She went directly into one of the cells, bare except for a single cot.

"I've led you to jail," she said, turning to him.

"As long as you don't leave me here." His hands unbuckled his pants.

"But I am going to leave you here," she said, taking off her clothes.

"Shut up," he said, reaching for her ass.

In the saloon, a drunken and confused Pancho Villa sat on a chair elevated by two aluminum camera cases, giving it the temporary stature of a throne. Beneath him drifted a bored and mostly stoned crowd of whores, actors, and mariachi players held together by the prevailing rumor that Wesley Hardin was in the process of flipping out and that they might be witnesses to a legendary event sure to be reported in *Rolling Stone*, *Time*, and *Cahiers du Cinéma*. This rumor was further reinforced by the appearance of the female star, who showed up full of righteous abuse about Wesley's deliberately sabotaging her career. In an unnaturally loud voice contracted from the still-rising effects of the pharmaceutical coke, Wesley had called her a self-indulgent cunt and a worthless actress who further and forevermore was living proof that the Spanish philosopher Ortega y Gasset was right when he said the twentieth century would see the final dominance of mediocrity over intelligence. Stunned and speechless by this reduction, the female star had returned to her hotel, where she had booked herself on the first flight to L.A.

Returning to the end of the bar, Wesley sat alone brooding about just what it was he had intended to do with this night. The rest of the saloon waited for him with awkward apprehension, no longer trying to pretend they were at a party or some kind of spontaneous *cinéma vérité* exploration by an aging master of the Western genre.

"We'll do the fucking mountain man scene," Wesley said as if startled by sudden illumination.

The mountain men were summoned and instructed to ask Pancho Villa how they could get laid now that they were his guests in Mexico. As Hank and Scarface approached the throne where Pancho Villa had passed out, the saloon door swung open and the producer swept in, followed by a newly arrived studio executive from L.A. in jeans and white Peruvian peasant's shirt. He was obviously thrilled to be on the front of a real crisis on a real set. Wesley ignored them, instructing the cameraman to keep on shooting.

Hank pulled on Pancho Villa's foot: "Pancho, now that we have fought and died for you, we would like to ask you a favor."

Pancho Villa, startled and confused, looked down at the kneeling mountain man: "Favor?...I don't need no favor. I have an occupation...ask him."

He pointed to Wesley, who explained his role to him: "You are Pancho Villa. *El jefe.* You must give the orders and make the decisions because within you lies the spirit of the people, for better or for worse. Not those profane assholes from Mexico City."

"Be like Anthony Quinn," Pancho Villa ordered. "Never say die, and ask for dollars, not pesos."

Wesley pointed to the producer: "The money man over here will give you one thousand dollars American."

Elated, Pancho Villa grabbed one of the whores and kissed her. "Then I take this *puta* and give you all the other *putas*. *Viva México!*"

A few cheers rang out from the crowd and the band swung into an enthusiastic version of "La Cucaracha." Wesley pointed at the cameraman to pan around the room to include the producer and the studio executive.

"Jesus Christ, Wes," said the producer. "This has gone far enough."

Wesley stood on a chair so that he was equal in height to the enthroned Pancho Villa. "These two men represent everything that's fucked up with this process," he said to a suddenly self-conscious Pancho Villa, who was looking for an easy way to get the whore down from his lap.

The drunken voice of the prop man sang out from behind the bar: "Hang the cocksuckers...burn 'em in phony receipts...."

The producer made a desperate move to grab the camera, but the cameraman, an ex-professional soccer player, eluded him easily, planting a quick kick to his groin while continuing to shoot.

The studio executive took this moment to step forward. "I plead with you, Mr. Hardin, to stop all of this. It's very upsetting to see a man of your legendary reputation lose all control in this manner."

"I am in total control," Wesley said calmly.

"Fire the son of a bitch," the producer gasped, kneeling on all fours.

The studio executive continued, raising his voice to include the entire saloon, "I must add that I represent the studio on this matter and the studio's position is that if this room isn't emptied in five minutes we will close the entire production."

The message communicated itself to the crowd, which grew suddenly subdued, all except the band, which misunderstood the silence and launched into "La Cucaracha" again.

"Keep on shooting, Sidney," Wesley said to the cameraman, who was in a nothing-left-to-lose mood.

"Put down that camera," the studio executive said.

"Why don't you tell him he'll never work again," Wesley said.

"All right. Put down that camera or you'll never work again."

"Keep shooting," Wesley said, as the crowd circled around them. "This is my set."

"Not any more, Mr. Hardin," the studio executive said, conscious that this historic moment was being filmed. "I am relieving you of that responsibility."

Wesley had almost reached the calm that he was seeking, needing only one more shock to cut him loose altogether. He took the .38 out of his belt and raised it, aiming toward the bottle on the bar that held the live tarantula. At that moment he saw Evelyn standing just inside the door, regarding him soberly. He lowered the .38, motioning for Sidney to hold the camera on her reaction. Then he fired, shattering the glass.

As one body, the crowd rushed out the door. All except for the studio executive, who walked over to the tarantula and squashed it with the heel of a custom-made English boot. "That's it," he said directly into the camera, managing to look both official and compassionate. "That's the whole ball of wax." Then he turned and left the saloon, nodding politely to Evelyn as he went through the swinging doors.

Shaken and exhausted, Wesley sat down at a table, Evelyn coming over to him and absently rubbing the back of his neck.

"Give me a two shot uptight and we'll call it a day," Wesley said to Sidney and the sound man, who were the only other people left in the saloon. "Assemble the footage in L.A. and consider yourself both on the payroll. Perhaps we'll continue this little exercise later on."

Having run out of all other options, Sidney raised the camera and focused on Wesley as he pulled Evelyn onto his lap. She put a hand up to block the lens but Wesley gently lowered it. "How would you feel about driving to Mazatlán tonight?" he asked. "We'll lie on the beach for a few weeks and see where we go from there."

"I would like that," she said, kissing him on the mouth.

Cut to A.D. and Walker rolling down the mountains in a second-hand Dodge van, their first stop a national park campsite a mile off the main road. They were on arid tableland, around them twisted formations of rock, a maze of natural arches and bridges bathed in a hard crimson and yellow evening light. They made a rough camp with the equipment and supplies they had bought after leaving Caleb's. A.D. wasn't going to pull his weight, that was obvious as he sat in front of the small fire Walker had made and played a few desultory notes on a pocket harmonica. Walker didn't mind, preferring to handle the chores himself, peeling potatoes and frying two steaks over the fire. After they had finished eating, Walker decided to tell A.D. what was on his mind.

"I'm ready to go my own way," he said. "You can have the van and I'll split at the next town where there's a bus station."

"No way, José," A.D. said. "You can't quit on me like some out-of-town roadie."

"I'm not up to doing the script."

"Who cares what you're not up to doing? If you sign for pay you got to play. I want to grab some of the movie pie. Anyway, you owe me for my eye. If it wasn't for you I'd be making my normal moves."

Walker didn't reply. Picking up the paper plates, he threw the steak bones into the darkness and the plates on the fire.

A.D. reached into his duffel bag and took out a bottle of Johnny Walker and took a long pull. "My days as a backup man are over. I been a backup man all my life, one way or the other. No way, José."

"Who is this José?" Walker asked.

The question infuriated A.D. "What are you, some kind of off-the-curb arrangement you don't know the way people speak any more? They must have rung your bell over there. Who is José? José is you, baby, and me and all the fucking people. José is José. What went down over there that you lost it so bad? You must have booked yourself into some kind of religious act. The street is where it's at now and how to get off it. Dash for cash."

Walker stood up and moved off toward the looming sentinels of rock.

"A deal like you only comes along once," A.D. yelled after him. "I'm staying with you rain or shine."

Walker turned back to him. "It'll never sell."

"Your old man will change that," A.D. said. "Your old man is an all-world pro who's done over thirty pictures and he knows how to move something off the lot."

"He has other problems," Walker said, turning away again toward the darkness.

A.D. reached into his duffel bag, producing a semi-automatic .22 pistol and a pocket tape recorder. "Sing me your song, mother fucker, or I'll blow a hole into you."

For the first time in days, perhaps weeks, Walker smiled. Then he walked off into the darkness and A.D. let him go. But A.D.

wasn't going to give up. He was going to mount one all-or-nothing assault. To do this he needed help in the form of a stash of morphine and speed he had stolen from the hospital and hidden in the back of the van. He built up the fire and made himself a goofball. Turning on the radio in the van as high as it would go, he found a C & W station and played along with Merle Haggard and Hank Snow on his harmonica. He sprinkled a little of the morphine into the fire as a kind of offering and settled back, waiting for the necessary focus to crystallize inside him. Then he searched for Walker.

"Walker? Walker?" A.D. yelled but there was no answer. He stumbled, falling to his knees, managing at the last minute to save the tape recorder. He turned it on: "I appreciate your intentions," Walker's voice said on tape. "They're better than mine because they mean to communicate whereas I'm pulled into myself and stuck in the swamp of my own experience...."

He turned the tape recorder off.

Walker sat barely fifty feet away hidden behind a huge boulder. He listened to the distant music on the radio and said nothing. But something did, in fact, feel lighter, as if a burden had been lifted inside him, a clenched fist that had somehow relaxed. He was inclined to let out the story, or a variation on the story, since there seemed to be so much pressure toward that end and since he had, in fact, helped create the situation. But he said nothing, feeling relieved that A.D. had decided to go off on his own.

"That shuts it then," A.D. said. Standing up, he fired a few shots to finalize the deal, the bullets richocheting off the rocks.

He had gone ten steps when Walker's voice stopped him. "You just shot me in the leg. I think it was on the rebound and it doesn't feel too serious."

A.D. sprinted toward Walker's voice, moving among the jagged rocks like a crazed broken-field runner.

Walker lay sprawled on his back, his right thigh matted with blood. A.D. ripped Walker's pants with two quick tears.

"It's not bad," he said, working quickly. "A flesh wound. Two bounces before it hit you. Don't worry about nothing. I was a medic in the navy."

He tore up his shirt into thin strips and tied them expertly around the wound. "If you're freaked I can get you into a hospital or rob a drugstore. There's always a way. But like I say, it's a scratch."

He drifted off, shifting down from the adrenaline and the sudden confrontation of three hundred mgs of diethylpropion hydrochloride with two healthy snorts of morphine.

"I'm going to pass on the drive," Walker said, beginning to notice how stoned A.D. was. "Maybe you could help me to the fire."

A.D. swayed to his feet and offered Walker a hand, and together they made their way back, Walker leaning heavily on A.D.'s shoulder. Once they fell, Walker's head scraping against a rock and opening a gash across his forehead. A.D. ripped up what was left of his shirt and tied a loose bandanna across Walker's head, partially blocking his vision. They moved on, toward a glow of embers where the fire had died down and where they could hear a disco beat from the radio.

"Hold your fire, we're coming in!" A.D. yelled. "We're behind our own lines and this is as safe as it's going to get." A.D. lost himself in a low maniacal giggle. "And you and I, Walker, are going to put it out on the table because neither of us has been dealing with a full deck."

He dragged an air mattress out of the van and helped Walker to shift himself on top of it, making him comfortable with a blanket and pillow. Then he stripped the bandages off Walker's leg and cleaned his wound with a fresh handkerchief, working away at each clot of blood as if it were a world unto itself. He topped it all off by pouring enough whiskey over the exposed area so that Walker almost lost consciousness.

"Now, now," A.D. whispered, pouring two large lines of morphine onto a pocket mirror and producing a cut-off straw from his pocket. "Snort on this here coup de grace, old buddy."

Walker did as he was told, content to lie back and be administered to, watching A.D. build up the fire and open a can of chicken soup to heat over the Coleman stove.

"Suppose we slip on back to what used to be," A.D. said after he had spoon-fed Walker the chicken soup, and the morphine was taking hold as they lay on their backs pinned to the vast night sky. "I believe it was Jim and his wife, Lacey, looking for sister Clementine who had stepped off the curb in India, or was it Bali?"

"India," Walker murmured. The soft sweet smell of his own species' shit was what he had noticed first and the freak-out of having one of his bags stolen by a stoned and starving French hippie dressed as a sadhu in a torn dhoti and shaved head. From that first ludicrous moment he had experienced a violent fear of and estrangement from the whole place that was never really to leave him, whereas his wife, to her amazement as well as his, had immediately felt the opposite, as if she had finally found her true home.

"As I recollect the story," A.D. said dreamily, pushing the button on the tape recorder, "Jim and Lacey were slugging on each other right from the bell. Their whole scene was on the rocks except for an occasional wrathful fuck, which is what we open up on, but both of them are too guilty and uptight to cop to it. Lacey didn't want to go to India in the first place because she felt too attached to her social scene, but she sure as hell wasn't going to let Jim go because a part of her knew that once he got away, that was it, going going gone and no matter how much she might want to see him cut up in little pieces and scattered to the wind, it was her that was going to walk out the door, not him.... And Jim, he was looking for a way to cut loose and he wanted to go quick before Clem came back, because all the time he never really thought she was in danger, just off on some adventure and not telling the old man was her way of telling herself she was on her own. He didn't like working for his old man, didn't like his friends, didn't like his car, didn't like his house, didn't like the second-rate mistress he had stashed in Chicago, in fact, he didn't like his whole shot... he was that strung out with himself.... How does that sound?"

"I suppose it was a little like that," Walker said softly, not able really to remember. "More or less like that... except there were the pleasures... the terrifying pleasures, running from one to the other, and always money, piling up money, making deals, always that... obsession with the next high roll... manipulating."

"Where would we cut to from the last scene?" A.D. asked, trying to push it along, resisting an impulse to let the stars devour him. "You remember that weird scene in the bedroom where they were in the middle of packing and going at each other, throwing things and screaming out all the hate and then that last roll on the rug...?"

After a long moment where it appeared that he had dozed off, Walker began to get into it:

RIGHT — TO INDIA... *Lacey opening her eyes and staring at a large fan turning slowly above her. She would be lying on a single bed and you can tell by the vacant expression in her eyes that she has no idea where she is as we go with her point of view: wicker furniture, cool blue and white tiles on the floor, the chaos of their clothes and luggage spilled around the room as if caught in a violent wind, an empty gin bottle lying on the pillow.... She stands on the balcony in her dressing gown, looking down at an ivy-colored brick wall surrounding a controlled garden with flowers, peacocks, bowing waiters, and a highly theatrical show business yogi performing a series of flashy asanas for the hotel guests sitting at tables on the lawn, one of whom is her hung-over and bored husband.... Dismissing the predictable view beneath her, she gazes enamored at the street beyond the hotel enclave where two elephants pass like ponderous ships through a congested stream of people, cows, water buffaloes, taxis, buses....*
EXTERIOR — MIDDAY... *riding in a hand-drawn ricksha down a narrow side street. Jim is appalled and depressed at the poverty, while Lacey, surprisingly, has nothing but enthusiasm for the languid exotic atmosphere. Suddenly he lashes out at her, telling her to keep her banal responses to herself and not try to insist imperially that he see things her*

way and to leave him the fuck alone. In this alienated mood they arrive at a simple one-story house with a tin roof surrounded by palm trees....
INTERIOR — HOUSE... *the melancholy sound of a vina and the tap-tap of a murdang, a long double drum. A dark-skinned woman in a maroon sari opens the door and they can see a large white room with a rug on the floor where an ancient white-bearded man in a starched dhoti interrupts the student playing the murdang and demonstrates how he wants the phrase played. He speaks in Tamil to one of the students, a handsome youth in his early twenties, but the young man, Samendra, is distracted by the appearance of the bizarre Westerners, in particular, Lacey. The teacher, Baba, takes a long stick with a black lacquer handle and whacks Samendra over the head, speaking to him reproachfully. Samendra bows, stands up, and walks over to Jim and Lacey. "Baba asks why you have interrupted the lesson?" Jim tells him the whole rap about Clementine and how they're looking for her and how worried they are and Samendra says all this in Tamil to Baba and he gives a reply which Samendra translates: "Baba says music was not your sister's true path. She was not a good student and Baba regrets having included her in his class." Jim interrupts to ask if Clementine is okay, if she's still alive, and Baba turns to him and states in highly theatrical Oxfordian English: "I do not care nor am I interested in what happened to your sister after she left my tutelage. Samendra will confess all he knows after his lesson is over. If you will excuse me, I am an old man and have no time for chatter."... He turns his back. Samendra manages to whisper that he will meet them on the beach....*
EXTERIOR... *They walk across the street to a wide spectacular beach facing the Bay of Bengal. It is hot and little waves of heat rise off the sand. In the distance, ebony-colored fishermen in loincloths pull their nets toward the shore. They are in the middle of an argument about why Jim didn't insist on knowing if at least Clementine was alive. He refuses to go back, saying that the place gave him the creeps and it's not going to make any difference anyway. She turns angrily away, only to fall back toward him, startled by a solitary figure staring at them with a coldly detached gaze not ten feet away. His naked body is covered with white ash and he*

holds a small three-pronged trident in his right hand. They have another argument about whether they should move down the beach and then…
SAMENDRA ARRIVES…*Looking at the sadhu, he gives him a coin and claps his hands. The sadhu takes the coin but doesn't walk away. "I could not leave," Samendra says, sitting down opposite them on the sand. Anticipating Jim's inevitable question, he says that as far as he knows Clementine is in New Delhi and that he can give them an address. It is obvious by the shy hesitant way he mentions Clementine's name that he is strung out on her. "She was not a bad student but she had no real interest in music. She quite severely damaged her hand, you know." They didn't know. "Yes, yes," he goes on rapidly. "She was in a taxi and there was a flat and as they were changing the tire the jack slipped. Her hand was on the ground and she just left it there for the car to crush. Quite amazing the way she left her hand there. I watched it myself."… They sit facing slightly different directions as if they had lost their connections with each other, the sadhu staring straight at them as before.… Jim asks: "What happened with her? I mean, I always knew she was using Indian music as a hustle to have an adventure, to break away for a while, but this is very extreme."… Samendra smiles at them. "Before the, ah, accident," he says, averting his eyes and staring off at the sea, "your sister was visiting a man who sat with Ramana Maharsi, the enlightened being from Arunachala whose body has now left us. This man, Chandra Doss, who sat with Ramana Maharsi for six years, is not a swami or anything like that. He is a simple man who has a family and sells bidis, these little cigarettes, in the marketplace. You can see him there anytime. He makes all these bidis and he sells them. Your sister met him because that is where she bought her cigarettes and she began to talk with him. Everything was falling apart for her and she thought that she might have to return home and Chandra Doss told her that it was true that everything was falling apart and that it would get worse no matter what she did and that she should embrace that state rather than deny it; what Ramana Maharsi calls the Atma-Vichara, to inquire intensely after the self. And so she inquired intensely after her self because that was what she was doing anyway, although in a very ignorant way,*

and soon all she was left with was the chaos of her own thoughts. Then Chandra Doss told her to say neti neti, or, no, not those thoughts either, and that is where perhaps the real crises began because she could not accept the existence of the Aham-Brahman." "The Aham-Brahman?" Lacey asks, bewildered by this explanation which has been spoken very fast, as if Samendra wants to get it all said so that he can just split. "Yes. Yes. The I. The absolute. The noise of her own mind brought a kind of madness upon her."…"You mean she flipped out?" Jim asks impatiently. Samendra appears pained, as if Jim is being purposely obtuse, which he no doubt is. But Samendra proceeds anyway. "One might say that your sister became gradually obsessed with the awareness that she was not her thoughts. I was a witness. I was there every day to watch. She would not talk to Baba about her music. She would not respond. She would not practice. Her whole life seemed to stop."…"What does that mean, she's not her thoughts?" Jim asks, almost shouting. "Of course she's her thoughts. Cogito ergo sum, baby."… Samendra stands up, frightened and embarrassed by the aggression in Jim's eyes. He turns away as if he cannot bear it any more, then suddenly whirls around to face them. "Tat-tvam-asi," he shouts, his face beaming as if he has remembered a magic formula. Sitting down, he smiles at them sweetly. "Tat-tvam-asi. Thou art that. That is what your sister began to meditate on. I remember that quite clearly. Of course I do not know what it all means because I am not sannyas. I am a musician. Perhaps you should ask Chandra Doss about the teaching of the great sage of Arunachala."…"She's become some kind of freak," Jim says quietly. They sit there silently until suddenly Samendra laughs and claps his hands. "You see, your sister discovered she could not control her thoughts for one second. That is something that we know here that you in the West are perhaps ignorant of."… Jim stands up to leave. "I don't know how to deal with that…. No, no." Samendra jumps up to stand beside him. "I seriously doubt whether you can stop your mind for one brief moment."…"Why should I stop my mind?" Jim asks. "I need all I can get out of it."…"I don't think that's an unreasonable request," Lacey says. "After all, it's what Clementine was obsessed by."…"I'm not in the mood for mystical parlor games," Jim says, nodding to Samendra. "In any case, I appreciate all this information. At least we know she's off on her own adventure and doesn't need us showing up looking for her."... Confused and insulted, Samendra bows and walks across the beach to the house.... "I think we should still try to find her," Lacey says on the way back to the hotel. "Obviously she's in an extremely perilous place."..."Who isn't in a perilous place?" Jim says. "Maybe she should find us."... They have a terrible fight on the street that ends with their walking off in separate directions....

CUT TO JIM WALKING DOWN THE STREET...so sunk in anxiety and despair that he barely notices a street festival of chanting pilgrims, snake charmers, sword swallowers, and acrobats. He passes a wooden platform where Kathakali dancers move through the rituals of an ancient myth with slow graceful gestures. One woman, her face divided into two colors, red and blue, laughs with one side of her face and cries with the other. He moves on, through screaming children throwing bags of water and urine. They surround him, taunting him, covering him with red dye, and drenching him with the awful fluid. He stands there helpless and enraged, unable to control himself....

LATER, HIS CLOTHES STILL DRENCHED...he finds himself before a cigarette stall on the corner of a busy thoroughfare. A small gray-haired man with most of his teeth missing sits on a rug at the rear of the stall sorting through a pile of handmade cigarettes. Jim stares at him, unable to approach. Several times he tries and the man waits expectantly, looking up at him. Jim glances at his watch, as if he has an appointment. Across the street pilgrims perform bathing rituals in a deep green pool in front of an ancient temple where women have spread out their laundry to dry on the stone steps. Monkeys chatter in the trees. A funeral procession passes, a child's body lying on a board covered with garlands of fresh flowers. "Time is a cruel master," the man says, but Jim can only nod. Finally he buys a pack of American cigarettes and leaves....

At this point, Wesley, sitting at a café on the beach at Mazatlán, stopped reading the typed transcript of Walker's tape even though there were more than a few pages remaining. It was past noon and he was on his third margarita and he felt slightly dizzy and more than a little hung over. Walking toward him on the beach were Sidney, the second unit cameraman, and Harold, a young producer from London sporting a new Panama hat and a Hawaiian shirt who had flown in the previous night and whose mission Wesley had somehow forgotten. He was not happy to see them. He needed time for his own thoughts, for this sudden permission he seemed to have granted himself toward an interior dialogue, or failing that, at least a period of refuge from the gleeful and vicious publicity he had received since his walkout and subsequent firing two weeks ago. "Neti, neti," he said aloud, realizing he knew nothing about Walker's mind and precious little about his own.

"You certainly chose a bucolic spot for yourself, Mr. Hardin," Harold said, maneuvering his bulk into a chair as he and Sidney sat down at the table.

He paused, trying to feel his way through the sullen atmosphere Wesley was projecting. The fact that he was in awe of the legendary director didn't help. Wesley sat immobile, his face half hidden underneath a peasant's straw hat, staring at the thick line of jungle where squads of green parrots kept up a raucous chatter. Inside the café the jukebox played Hank Williams to an empty room. After a lengthy silence, Harold tried again: "Your charming wife told me to tell you that she won't be joining us for lunch. She pleads guilty to a shopping compulsion directed toward native rugs."

Wesley said nothing, looking at Harold with a preoccupied frown until Harold was forced to look away. Sidney, on the other hand, didn't mind Wesley's mood, much as it seemed to match his own, and he waited until he had ordered a drink before he tried to bring the situation into some kind of focus.

"Harold might be able to come up with money to continue shooting. I filled him in this morning about the stuff we shot in Durango and those few scenes down here and the one with Evelyn on the fishing boat."

"Of course I have to look at the footage," Harold said. "But I'm thrilled with the whole concept. And I think a personal straight-from-the-guts exploration of a major crisis in a famous man's life has broad popular appeal."

"I was thinking just the opposite," Wesley said.

"Indeed?" Harold said. "Sidney gave me the impression you were quite excited about the way things were going."

"I don't want to think about results, which means I don't want to think about money, which means I don't want to consider turning what are essentially private notes into a feature film. I started shooting out of rage, just wanting to shove it up the studio's ass. I'm not interested in hustling my private life and I don't want anyone else doing it either."

"Then what am I doing here?" Harold asked.

"I don't know," Wesley said quietly. "And I don't want to know."

"Does that mean a wrap?" Sidney asked.

"For you it does."

Wesley watched a sailboat slowly coming about in the offshore breeze and felt himself to be in a kind of agony. He was either saying things that were too personal or not relevant at all.

"Are you considering other projects?" Harold was asking.

"I'm developing a script to be shot in India. A contemporary story about young Americans searching for themselves and finding the opposite."

"That seems a sweaty task," Harold said. "Sort of a producer's nightmare."

"I would rather read about it myself," Wesley admitted.

"Perhaps you don't want to work at all. Perhaps it's time for philosophy and rumination."

"Perhaps." Wesley rose slowly from his seat. Swaying slightly he looked down at them, his face stern and yet somehow fragile. "My store is not open, gentlemen. Either for personal little forays into my beleaguered psyche or for broad popular entertainment. But perhaps you can develop something between yourselves."

With that he left them, walking slowly down to the beach along the edge of the sea, his white linen pants rolled up past his ankles, his blue cotton shirt falling loosely over his waist. The air was heavy and moist and he walked in a slow shuffle through the sand. His body was no longer friendly to him. His joints ached and his breathing was shallow and he moved with no obvious purpose or direction. He could not remember a time when he wasn't involved in some project, either going toward or leaving behind. There had always been something to fasten on to, people around to keep him going, keep him on the point, pull him through. It was true that over the past decade he had come to take it all for granted, that he had in a sense just gone through the motions as developments formed around him from the accumulated weight of his professional presence. It was a somewhat startling fact that he was still functioning at all after more than thirty films in the can, that the inevitable damage to body, mind, and soul, although severe and now seemingly terminal, had been held in check enough for him to sustain a reputation as a safe and bankable director. There had always been a raw primitive edge to his work, a kind of sentimental passion that every once in a while would bring in gold from the box office. But all of that was gone now.

He took off his white linen jacket and lay down on the warm sand. But the noon light was hard and exhausting and abruptly he moved off the beach to sit in the shade of two giant palm trees. The light was softer and more diffuse and that pleased him. An awareness of light was what cushioned him when he approached a scene, what protected him from the mechanical boredom of the medium. But fuck light, he thought. He was headed for a black hole. The journey of his son toward the disappearance of his daughter reminded him of that. He resented having to read Walker's pages. It was a forced and unnatural arrangement, one that he shouldn't have initiated. But unfolding the remaining pages, he began to read anyway:

INTERIOR—DAY...*Jim walks through the hotel lobby, obviously distraught, his clothes torn and matted from the festival hi-jinks...As he picks up the key at the front desk, he is handed a slip of paper from Samendra with Clementine's address in New Delhi.... Entering his room he reaches for a bottle of Scotch on the dresser. The curtains are drawn against the late afternoon sun and Lacey is sleeping, curled in on herself as if for protection. She opens her eyes, regards him. "Could you come into bed and just hold me for a minute?" she asks.... He takes a long pull from the bottle and steps out of his clothes before he answers: "I have to get into the shower. I'm covered with piss and slime and probably have about*

three months to live." He disappears into the bathroom. . . . As he's stand-
ing under the shower Lacey enters beside him and starts soaping his back,
kissing him on the shoulder. "I get panicked when you get weird and ag-
gressive." She reaches around his waist and takes hold of his cock. "I need
an adventure," she says, squeezing him gently. . . . He shuts his eyes as her
soapy fingers surround him. "What kind of an adventure?" He turns her
around and lifts one of her legs so that he can slide into her. "Any kind as
long as it's new," she whispers as he slowly begins to move inside her. . . .

(I'm stopping here to say, who are you, Pop, and why are we
indulging in this devious contract? Somehow, wherever Clementine is, she would probably find our attention unnecessary, even
distasteful. She never needed your approval, for one thing, at least
not as much as I did and still do. And then, too, she might not want
to be found. It's as if you and I are both in a waiting room and need
to pass time while we wait for our separate exits. But Clementine
might not be in the waiting room, at least not this one. She might
have stepped outside altogether. But we can't let her go, can we?
And I can't let you go, nor you me, no matter how much we might
want to release each other. So send money and I'll send pages. Post
the next check to General Delivery, Salt Lake City, and add expense money and whatever paternal bonus you might be able to
spare. We're traveling through Utah, angling toward Nevada. I had
a slight accident with my leg so the healing process has been interrupted but nothing serious. The process within is another story. But
one positive aspect to our contract is that it gives me a slice of time
to deal with culture shock while I unravel my own back story. I'm
grateful for that even if it means confronting death and separation
and a few other essential questions that I have no answers for. . . . By
the way, your instincts about A.D. Ballou, if instincts is the right
word, proved to be shrewd and on the point. Without his relentless ambition to find a slot in the movie biz I would never have the
edge or perversity to continue, and as it is, of course, I might fade

at any moment. I have to threaten you with that from time to time as that is what you inevitably threaten me with. Although Mr. Ballou, for one, is determined to bring all the elements together. But from what I hear on TV and read in the papers, any future projects you might conceive are strictly in the realm of fantasy. Is it true that the head of M-G-M has been quoted as saying as far as he's concerned you've "misdirected your last film"? Perhaps you think an independently financed film will rescue you, but I can promise you that India doesn't rescue anyone. It's like the movie business in that way.... Did you notice how I controlled the scenes for you, keeping the exteriors to a manageable minimum so the background doesn't devour the foreground? And the sex is mostly in easy close-ups where you'll be able to shoot interiors out of the country if the censors bother you, which they will. All of this sounds as if I think you're going to go over there. I don't really. Evelyn told me that you think you're dying, but I told her you always say that and probably what happened was that you stumbled for a brief moment on your own inhibited sense of impermanence....Waiting for your next installment...Walker.)

WESLEY stood up and folded the pages, putting them back in his pants pocket. Then he walked down the beach and slowly climbed the stone steps that wound their way up a steep hill to a clearing overlooking the entire coast. Wesley's house was one of several in various stages of construction scattered about on the periphery of the clearing and mostly obscured by thick jungle foliage. The entire compound was the dream and obsession of Sam Colson, an ex-San Francisco restaurateur, sometime actor and movie impresario, who had bailed out of a potential business scandal by sinking all his funds and cash flow into a south-of-the-border real estate venture called Vivi la Viva. Wesley had known Senor Viva, as he was locally called, for over twenty years and had used the compound before when there was only Sam's house and a guesthouse with a thatched roof and no running water. After he had separated from his third wife, Wesley had stayed for over five months, sleeping, drinking, and reading all of Conrad before going back to L.A. and doing everything all over again. But these days the compound had a more worldly vibration, being mostly inhabited by a loose mélange of high-class drug dealers, movie people, radical lawyers and their more infamous clients, well-heeled social drifters from L.A. and New York, and the odd surprise wandering in off the beach, all of whom Wesley preferred to avoid. Except for Sam, who lay watching him from a hammock as good as naked in a pair of bikini briefs barely visible among the folds of his ample stomach, a pair of round dark glasses perched on the end of his soft and fleshy nose. He offered Wesley a sip of his gin and tonic.

"You have to put in an elevator," Wesley gasped, wiping his face with his shirt sleeve and taking the gin and tonic. "I can't make the steps any more."

"Forget the steps. I haven't been down those steps in six months. Longer. When you get to be our age life has to become a series of well-arranged retreats."

Wesley collapsed into a low-slung beach chair, staring up at Sam's patriarchal presence. "My life is more a rout than a retreat." Suddenly he felt irritated. "You read those pages?"

"Of course I read those pages. Evelyn had them Xeroxed and she gave them to me. How do you expect me not to read those pages? I know both your demented children. I even, if you recall, tried to have ingress with your daughter at a particularly precarious moment in my life."

"So you did," Wesley admitted.

"And as for Walker, no matter how twisted and deluded he might be, I'm sure he doesn't expect you to go over to India and shoot some crappy mystical adventure story that involves your own kids."

"Why not? It's a good hook. It's personal. Motivated."

"You've never done anything personal in your life. And who

knows where your motivations spring from. I speak to you as a friend. You should quit. Actually, you have quit. If you come back in the ring, you're going to get your head knocked off."

Wesley drained the rest of Sam's drink. "I don't really care about winning and losing any more. But I'm probably too compulsively theatrical and ignorant to do nothing."

"Not theatrical," Sam said, swinging his fat legs over the hammock and peering down at Wesley. "Too attached to all the bullshit."

Sam refilled the glass with the gin from a thermos tucked into the rear of the hammock. Taking a drink, he handed the glass to Wesley and went on. "One option is to consciously bury yourself alive in a beautiful, incestuous patch of paradise such as this one. Although I strongly suspect that when you finally approach the angel of death all suntanned and distracted, you might find yourself in the coldest hell, such would be your accumulation of rage, fear, and remorse."

"I'd make that deal," Wesley said. "One moment being equal to another. Except that I've fouled all my nests, including this one."

"What a pity. I was so looking forward to sabotaging our sunset years together."

Sam pulled a black silk kimono around him and together the two old friends walked across the clearing down a soft and verdant path decorated on either side with Japanese rock and flower arrangements, a narrow plunging waterfall, and a shaded grotto used mostly for midday drugs and backgammon. They stopped in front of Wesley's house, a wood and concrete cantilevered form sweeping out over a steep cliff facing the Pacific.

Wesley hesitated, not wanting to go inside. "I'm sliding," he said and sat down on a curved stone bench. "I won't be around this time next year."

Sam let his bulk come to rest on the stone bench. "That's entirely possible, although it could be your mind that's on the slide."

"It's my heart, actually. And certain key pores in my skin which seem to leak energy and a certain, I don't know, essential juice. I'm finished, Sam, and that's not a bad thing to know. It's a kind of relief."

"If this is your way of saying that you're going to India, then I agree with you."

Wesley fumbled through his jacket pocket for a cigarette. "Not India, not Mexico, not L.A. ever again. In fact, why don't you use the house on Mulholland and take a break from all this Shangri-La stuff? You're as stuck in your fun as I am."

For the first time Sam looked at his friend with real concern. "I might do that. But you'll need a foxhole. You can't just hang out at resorts and film festivals."

"I still have my father's place. Or at least I think I do. Off the coast of Labrador."

"What about Evelyn?"

"I don't know about Evelyn these days," Wesley said. "But I would hope she'd come with me. She's from up there. The north anyway."

Sam started to leave, then turned back toward Wesley and said: "I say fuck 'em all; your kids, your wife, whatever's left of your career, even your friends. You want to leave, go ahead. You want to pull the plug on yourself, do yourself in, that's okay. Take what you have left to do and do it. No one cares anyway."

Then he continued down the path and Wesley went inside.

Closing the door, Wesley moved toward the distant sound of the Beach Boys singing "Good Vibrations." He stopped at the end of the *entrada*, looking at the blue tiles on the floor of the clean white living room and through the open glass doors to the wooden deck, where Evelyn lay naked on a towel. A thin bearded man, also naked, was slowly rubbing suntan oil onto her back. He had shut his eyes as if willing all his energy to the ends of his fingers. There was something about the harsh light bouncing off the white walls and Evelyn lying so boldly on her stomach with her thighs slightly parted that reminded Wesley of another scene. Perhaps it was Godard's *Contempt*, with Brigitte Bardot stretched out on a stone parapet, her body silhouetted against the warm blue of the Mediterranean. Or was it an image from one of his own films of a floating daydream? Fritz Lang, at the end of his life, had played himself in Godard's film; an old director, burdened with too much cynical wisdom, trying to promote one last project. Other directors had turned an occasional trick, John Huston had acted, as had Von Stroheim and Welles and Nick Ray. But their performances embarrassed him because he could never do it.

He watched the hand on Evelyn's back work its way upward, pausing briefly on top of her head before wandering gently toward the cheeks of her ass. Resting there, a middle finger slid slowly down and probed deeper. As Evelyn shifted her rump to welcome the invasion, Wesley walked forward and the bearded man raised his head, his eyes a startling blue. Wesley moved slowly, giving the man time to stand up, while Evelyn, sneaking a look beneath her arm, preferred to remain as she was.

"Good afternoon, Mr. Hardin," the man said, reaching for his bathing trunks. He had a soft pouting face and curly blond hair; Wesley marked him for an actor or beach hustler.

Wesley stepped up to him, eyes narrowed. "It's like Texas down here in the sense that no one cares much if a man kills another man for porking around with his wife."

The man tried hard to be charming: "I am French and unaware of such rules."

Wesley slapped him on the side of the head with an open palm.

He hadn't hit a man in forty years and the sudden violence shocked him. The Frenchman seemed more embarrassed than hurt, even somewhat concerned, as if Wesley had made himself vulnerable to a stroke.

He stepped backwards, watching Wesley. "It was a small hedonistic interlude, Mr. Hardin, nothing more."

"I'm sure," Wesley said and turned to face the sea.

"He didn't mean anything serious," Evelyn said after the man had left. "He works in the French consulate in Mexico City and comes down here to fish."

"I don't care about any of that," Wesley said. "I was reacting to something else."

Evelyn sat up and wrapped her arms around her knees while Wesley took off his shirt and sat down next to her on an aluminum beach chair. His skin was shockingly pale next to hers, hanging loose and old from his ribs, never to be firm again.

"I might go to New York," he said, looking out over the railing toward the parallel line of the horizon. "There's private financing available for the Indian film, at least according to my agent. Perhaps you want to stay here or go on a trip. Maybe Yucatán or Guatemala. You haven't seen any of the Aztec stuff. "

"You don't want me with you," she said flatly.

He avoided her eyes and she stood up and walked over to the edge of the deck. Then she bent down and picked up the tape deck where the Beach Boys were singing "Fun, fun, fun 'til her daddy takes the T-bird away!" and hurled it over the cliff where it shattered on the rocks below. When she turned to face him, her eyes were openly angry. He had never seen her lose control this way and he watched her closely, grateful for the small rush of anxiety that had awakened inside him, for the hint, however slight, that the wall surrounding his heart might have a few expanding cracks in it.

"I don't want you involved in my internal melodramas," he said, trying to provoke her even more.

But she didn't back down. "You use dead or alive like a club. Maybe there's something simple that you've forgotten."

"Are you telling me to shit or get off the pot?"

"I'm telling you that when you married me you didn't know whether you could go on. That's what you said then; that you had had this heart attack, that you were burned out and had outlived yourself. I thought you took me with you because you knew I would help you when your time came."

She watched him now, because she had never talked to him like this. She expected him to turn away and he did, but then he turned back to her, his eyes strangely moist and alive.

"What was in the deal for you when you took up with me?" he asked.

"I would have taken any deal to get out of Labrador, not that you're just any deal. I was thirty and I thought I was in my slot forever. The most I could hope for was a trip to St. John's or Labrador City. I never told you I was going to marry someone else. Way before you found me. When you asked me to go with you I had to go. He understood, but if he had run into you he would have killed you. You know how those boys from Goose Bay are."

"Do you have regrets?" he asked.

"Not too many, most of the time. He married someone else and went to Sudbury to work in the mines. I thought I loved him. That's something else I learned I don't know anything about."

"Would you come to Labrador with me?"

"Probably."

"Because you owe me?"

"I suppose."

He sighed. His legs hurt and his feet were cold and he was very tired. Evelyn leaned over and rested her head on his lap.

"Did you read Walker's script?" he asked.

"Yes, and then I gave it to Sam and he read it. He says Walker's off the deep end and you're crazy to indulge him."

"What do you think?"

"I'd like to know what comes next."

He shut his eyes, but before he could fall asleep she had helped him into the bedroom. Lying naked on the bed, he felt her lips wander softly over his weary and aching body and then her fingers massaged the soles of his feet until he slept. She lay beside him for a long time before she dressed and took a taxi into town, where she spent the afternoon shopping for a new tape deck and finishing what she had begun with the Frenchman from Mexico City.

AFTER A.D. had dressed Walker's wound and they had gotten stoned enough to sleep for a few hours, they drove down off the high mountain plateau in the early morning light and headed north toward Salt Lake City, where they stopped at a Holiday Inn on the outside of town. A.D. ordered a few drinks from room service and checked Walker's wound again, bathing and hovering over him like an anxious nurse, so much so that Walker finally yelled that he wanted to sleep. A.D. sighed, tucking him in once more before he went outside for a walk alongside the state highway that shot like a smoky arrow into the heart of the city. He was filled with terror that he might have been trying to kill Walker. He had always managed to abuse or self-destruct his own ambitions as if a stubborn force inside him was determined not to let him ever switch tracks or hustle a new deal. Walking around the front of a newly built super-market, he knelt down on the asphalt behind several produce trucks and vowed then and there not to blow this opportunity or betray himself, no matter what. When he returned to the motel Walker was awake, sitting on the edge of the bed fully dressed.

"Let's head for Nevada," Walker said. "We have a few thousand to play with. Maybe we'll get lucky and walk away from movieland."

"No way," A.D. said with sudden vehemence. "The only way you're going to walk away from movieland is when we complete the deal."

"Let's just get to Nevada," Walker repeated, hobbling for the door.

In three hours they had crossed through the shimmering white hallucinations of the Great Salt Lake Desert and pulled into the parking lot of the Red Garter Casino, a few hundred yards across the state line. After they had checked into a room, they went di-rectly to the tables. They played steadily and morosely, oblivious of time, occasionally passing each other without expression as they changed tables or took a break in the brightly lit twenty-four-hour luncheonette. Once Walker stepped outside to smell the cool desert air. It was night and above him a hundred-and-fifty-foot red, white, and blue cowboy pointed a finger toward the action, signaling "This Is the Place" to a convoy of four Mack trucks groaning in from the desert. The parking lot was alive with cowboys and Indians and Winnebagos from every state. Walker felt an urge to join a herd of tourists filing into a Greyhound bus after an hour's pit stop in front of the slot machines. He had enough money. He could get off after a few hundred miles, maybe in Oregon. Rent a little house, phone it in to the old man simple and straight, just the facts about Clem. But of course he went back inside. He lost steadily and when he was down to his last two hundred dollars he went back to the room and tried to sleep.

A.D., on the other hand, was on a roll. He had moved around the room, stopping here and there, shooting a little craps, dropping a hundred, winning two, not doing anything at roulette, breaking even at blackjack. Then he got reckless and bored at roulette and hit a couple of straight numbers and he was a grand up. He changed from five- to twenty-five- to fifty-dollar chips and kept on playing. He lost and then he won and won again, big, twenty one-hundred-dollar chips on number twenty-three. It was as if the hand of God had reached down and dropped a gold chip on his lap. He was up fourteen grand. He decided to keep four for himself and give the rest to Walker as payment for the next installment of the script, making himself the producer. He would have Walker sign a paper saying all three of them owned the script equally. This was his move. He would have half a script credit along with the producer's credit, and if Wesley pulled out they could take it to a younger director more able to deal with action. Because if there was one thing A.D. felt the script needed it was action. Or another character. If there was another person along, another girl perhaps, a friend of Lacey's that Jim could fall in love with, then sex would be better and more complicated and there would be more angles. Later he would deal with all of that. For now he would just shine it on.

He cashed in his chips, except for a hundred dollars' worth of ones, and put Walker's ten grand into a separate pocket in a sealed envelope. Then he went over to the blackjack table and spent the next several hours neither winning nor losing.

Meanwhile, Walker, who hadn't been able to sleep, was trying to wear himself out by returning to the script. He had been working off and on, occasionally watching the action in the casino for a few minutes, but mostly hanging around the desk while the scene built up inside him and he felt himself pulled back to that long traumatic journey by train up the length of India to New Delhi. It was the smoky evening light in the Madras train station that he remembered first and then the babble of thousands of voices....

EXTERIOR — MIDDAY... *Coming in over the scene with a crane shot of Jim and Lacey following two porters bent double under twelve pieces of luggage as they make their way through a chaos of travelers, beggars, and food vendors. The exotic anarchy of the scene has drawn them closer together. They certainly look more cooled out than they did a few days ago, wearing white cotton kurtas that hang loosely over their waists and newly bought leather sandals. As the porters place their luggage in their first-class compartment, Jim whispers to Lacey in a broad imitation of an Indian accent, "It doesn't matter if all of India is outside wanting to come in. I mean, does it now? We are inside and being inside is all that matters when one experiences the outside in such an aggressive worldly manner. I don't know if that is properly philosophical, young lady, but I'm very much fatigued, not just physically, but in my own spiritual body as well and as we know, weariness admits to its own demands."... This while sliding a hand under her flowing kurta... the porters have laid out their bedrolls, accepted a tip, and left. The train picks up speed as it pulls out of the station. Through the window scenes of rural India: endlessly parched fields, smoke from a thousand cooking fires, cardboard and tin shacks outside of ancient mud villages where oxen push waterwheels and hollow-eyed children stare blankly at the passing train....*

THESE SCENES INTERCUT... *with Jim and Lacey cozy and intimate inside their protective cocoon, playing cassettes on their tape deck, drinking wine and eating sandwiches from a straw basket the hotel provided, making love.... Within the rhythm of the montage night arrives, then the first streaks of morning light across the flat dusty landscape.... The train stops at the crowded station of a small city. It's hot. They have an hour's wait and decide to stretch their legs on the platform outside where entire families live and sleep in the midst of the usual food vendors and comings and goings....*

ANOTHER ANGLE... *From inside a nearly empty restaurant an American couple, whom we know by their adopted Indian names of Sita and Bodhi, sip tea and silently watch Jim and Lacey as they stroll down the platform. They have been on the trail for a very long time and look utterly wasted in their torn and grease-stained lungis and kurtas, faded*

*prayer beads made of tulsi wood draped around their necks, their jaun-
diced faces sunken and empty-eyed. As Jim and Lacey reach the end of
the platform and turn back toward the train, three lepers appear like
apparitions from a grotesque dream, waving their open sores as they
ask for alms. An old woman with half her nose missing tries to rub a
hideous dripping arm across Lacey's shoulder. Lacey screams. Reaching
into her purse, she throws a handful of bills at the lepers, who crawl on
their hands and knees after more money than they've ever seen.... As
they make their way back to the train, Bodhi steps outside the restaurant
and intercepts them. He is a dark-haired young man with a long matted
beard and small oval eyes that seem too slow and controlled. "Those were
lepers," he says to Lacey. "You'll have to get rid of your shirt." Lacey, on
the edge of hysteria, starts to cry but Bodhi puts his hand gently on her
arm. "Don't worry. Happens all the time. Come on in and have a cup of
tea."...Numbly they follow him inside, sitting down next to Sita, who
is blond and perilously thin. "Put this on," she says to Lacey, taking a
wadded-up orange kurta out of her handbag and handing it to her....
"They never actually touched me," Lacey says.... "I know what I'm talking about," Sita says, her pale blue eyes insistent.... Obediently Lacey
changes into the torn and soiled kurta that makes her look as freaked as
she feels. "I have been inside that rag a long long time," Sita says softly.
"It carries my vibrations, and if you open up to them you'll relax." Lacey
nods, not wanting to pursue it any further. On the platform in front of
them an old man in a dhoti starts to play a srangi (Indian violin). He
is blind, and is helped by a young girl, who sings along in a high tender
voice. A few people drop coins in front of him.... "Going north, are you?"
Bodhi asks.... "New Delhi," Jim answers and then Bodhi gets right to
it. "Listen, brother, can you spare enough change for two poor pilgrims
to get on the train? We're going up to Rishikesh and we sort of lost it. I
picked up malaria in Cochin and both of us went through the hepatitis
trip. Any way you cut it, we're busted."...Jim offers him a wad of rupees.
With great deliberation, Bodhi counts out what is needed and hands the
rest to him. "Blessings on you for a pure and compassionate act." He calls
out for two orders of dumplings and kurds, then turns to stare at a young*

boy in a white Rolling Stones T-shirt trying to hustle a pack of Camels. "Hold on. Just wait right there. I see an old friend." He turns to Jim. "If you can front me three hundred more rups I can absolutely guarantee you a serene and expansive ride all the way up to the city of your choice, Nueva Del-hi."...Jim hands him the rupees and he walks quickly outside where he and the boy begin a transaction, obviously not for cigarettes.... Sita sighs. "He was beautiful in Mysore. He was very open, like a baby when we saw the Puri Baba. He cried and kissed his feet. It was a holy moment." She stares off across the tracks as they sit in the hot oppressive silence waiting for the train....

CUT TO...*four small black balls of opium in the palm of Bodhi's hand; in the background, through the train window, the setting sun sinks over bleak rolling hills. Bodhi passes everyone a ball. "The best, most efficient way is to shove it up your ass. But if you can't handle that you can swallow it."...He and Sita proceed to execute the first option. Jim swallows his but Lacey hesitates. "I've never done anything like this," she says with an awkward giggle.... "No one's forcing you," Bodhi says. "It just smooths and grooves a boring trip. Takes you off the clock."...Jim puts an arm around Lacey, pulls her to him. "C'mon, sweetheart, it's like a Perc or Valium."...Closing her eyes, she swallows the opium with a sip of wine.... Sita pours more wine into a copper offering bowl that rests on a makeshift altar set up underneath the train window; it's created from a yellow silk cloth laid cross the width of one of Jim's suitcases. She and Bodhi have made themselves at home, having claimed the upper two bunks for themselves. At the rear of the altar, on either side of a burning candle, are a smoking incense stick and an ancient skull bowl. A many-colored paper cutout of a mandala rests in front of the altar next to a bell and a sickle-shaped bone knife. On the window they've taped two photographs: a reproduction of the goddess Kali, her blue four-armed body standing triumphant over two headless corpses, and a black-and-white photograph of a ferocious smooth-skinned yogi covered with ash sitting naked underneath a banyan tree, his pupils raised upward so that only the whites of his eyes are visible.... Bodhi lies back on a lower bunk, his hands locked behind his neck, very relaxed and satisfied with the way* things are going. "Sita and I might do a little puja. Jump the energy level. Sanctify the space and pacify the demons."..."Well sure," Jim says. "Whatever it takes."... Sita, seated in a half lotus in front of the altar, nods and clasps the palms of her hands together, bowing slightly. Then she touches the top of her head and intones: "Om Hum Hrim Siva Sakti-byham Svaha."... Lacey curls up inside Jim's embrace as they lie on the opposite bunk. She can't stop giggling. "This is all a little theatrical, don't you think? A little bit hippie-dippy."... Sita turns to stare at her, a slow sad smile on her thin lips.... "I didn't mean anything," Lacey says. "I just don't know what's going on."... After a long pause, Bodhi says: "It's theatrical, all right. If you know that, you'll come through the dreams okay."..."Come through what dreams?" Jim asks, struggling to make sense through faculties that are spinning away from him.... "Whatever dreams Mother India has in store for you," Bodhi replies. "This country doesn't work, you understand. It doesn't want to work. It's in a time switch. Everything that's repressed back home is on the street here. The outside becomes the inside or is it the other way around? Certain things become available. Our guru teaches us not to shrink from the senses but to conquer them through experience. He says perfection can be attained by satisfying all desires. Take it right to the street, he says. Every event is sacred. That's our Baba's special message for you this evening. Just watch and accept. Every rip-off, betrayal, slimy surprise; they're all opportuni-ties to jump your level."..."What's he saying?" Lacey whispers to Jim. She is beginning to feel stoned and paranoid.... "Something occult, no doubt," he says. As if from a great distance they watch Sita ring a little brass bell, softly repeating a mantra: "Om Jaya vijaya vijaya."... Lacey tries to sit up but falls back on the bunk. "Oh, God," she moans. "What's happen-ing to me?"..."You're on hold," Bodhi explains, standing up and smiling down at them. "We dipped your opium into a little elixir of snake juice. Copped it from an old jungle Baba back at Goa. You'll be paralyzed for a few hours, nothing more than that." They watch him, unable to move or speak as he systematically goes through their luggage, emptying out Lac-ey's purse and Jim's wallet and trying on Jim's clothes. Sita remains ab-sorbed in meditation, her eyes half closed, the mantra a whisper through her lips…. "You're observers now," Bodhi goes on. "Tantric TV watchers. Pranayama is a great yoga. Very pure. Watching your breath and your thoughts and your money and possessions come and go."…He tries on one of Jim's white linen jackets, admiring himself in a hand-held mirror. Impatiently, Sita tells him to get on with it…. Bodhi sighs, folding up the jacket and putting it with the rest of his chosen wardrobe. "We have to complete the puja. We're on the sixth day of a seven-day puja devoted to getting Sita knocked up. We're neophytes, you understand, and a lot can go wrong when you're working the kundalini up the spinal column and touching base with all the chakras. That old inner woman can cause you grief if you don't stay on the point. So we have to perform when the moon tells us to perform. Tomorrow will be the fertile time for a god-child to be conceived. Now we store the energy, hold back the sperm until the auspicious moment, and then let the saki unite with Siva."…"Please," Sita implores…. "All right then," Bodhi says, turning back to Jim and Lacey for one final word. "Don't worry about your passports. We just want to meet our needs, nothing more. A few clothes, your money, tape deck, stuff you can easily replace. You're loaded, after all. Hey, we're not out to do anyone in. Although, as our Baba says, we occupy the places of the gross. But in his infinite compassion he gave us the tools to process it."…All this while he's quickly removing his clothes and joining Sita, who is sitting naked on a bedroll in front of the altar. They stare into each other's eyes with great seriousness, intoning "Hrim, Shrim, Kleem," as Lacey and Jim lie pinned to the bunk unable not to look…. Sita's fingers slowly circle the tip of his cock. His breathing becomes rapid as he squeezes Sita's nipples. For a moment they have to pull back, shutting their eyes as they regain control…. "We need music," he suggests…. Sita looks at him impatiently. "Don't be an asshole. Concentrate on the gap between breaths. Abandon yourself to those gaps. You remember what Baba says."…"I'm not keeping the Atma in mind," Bodhi says. "All I feel like doing is fucking your brains out…." She looks at him with disgust. "If you shoot your filthy load into me I'll never forgive you."…"No danger in that," he says, looking at his wilted cock…. "It's five minutes to twelve," Sita reminds him. "We've come too far to throw it away…." She bends down to give *him an efficient blow job. As he becomes erect she pulls away and slowly lowers herself toward him. But before she can settle herself over him, he ejaculates in short spasmodic bursts. "You creep," she cries out. "You've ruined everything." She turns away and bursts into tears. . . . A few hours later the train pulls into a dark and nearly deserted station. Jim and Lacey sleep the dreamless sleep of the drugged while Sita and Bodhi prepare to leave the compartment, looking resplendent in white linen suit and clinging silk dress, a gang of porters carrying all their bags except two, which they have left behind as a gesture of goodwill.*

After A.D. went through his stack of one-dollar chips he went back to the room and found Walker asleep. The pages were on the floor beside the bed. After A.D. read them, he wrote out a rough contract establishing that he had paid Walker ten thousand dollars and therefore was part owner of the script, along with Wesley, who up until then had paid out seventy-five hundred. Before he went to sleep he found a secretary in the casino's office to type up the contract in legalized English.

When Walker and A.D. found themselves awake at the same time, they ate, gambled for a few minutes, and drove down the road toward Las Vegas. It was night and the road was empty with calm humpbacked mountains on either side of them. After fifty miles of driving A.D. said, "I read the pages. Your old man is never going to go for that blow job. He's had John Wayne and those other righteous old dudes riding through his flicks."

"I owe him a blow job. He can do what he wants with it."

"Well, that's a family problem," A.D. said. "And I never mess with family problems, not even my own."

"We'll red line the scene," Walker said. "His films never get that close to sex, at least not the explicit kind."

"Whatever you say, partner," A.D. said, trying to promote his new image as skillful producer. "I don't want to turn off your flow. I'm just telling you that the script doesn't altogether play for me.

If Jim and Lacey could take up with one of those weird hippies in the train and get themselves into a steamy triangle, then you'd have yourself a hook. I'd follow a hook like that into deep water, especially if you had two women on either side of the sandwich. And I'm not a deepwater man."

"The main characters are pretty well set."

"Does that mean you're sticking to what went down over there? Because if you are, we might have trouble moving this one off the lot."

"The facts have to be somewhere in the room or the old man won't pay attention."

"Herd them into the corner," A.D. said. "Out of the story's way."

They stopped at a small hotel-casino in Ely, a run-down mining town halfway to Las Vegas. Over apple pie and coffee A.D. produced the contract for Walker to sign.

"You're making your move," Walker said, looking over the contract.

"It's now or never," A.D. said. "And I'm taking my inspiration from the now jar."

"Who do you see in the middle of this triangle you've set up?" Walker asked. "Me, you, or the old man?"

"In a triangle there's only a middle if you start to lose," said A.D., who had no idea what he was really saying. "And that won't happen."

"I assume you've contacted a top lawyer?"

"Out of L.A. and on the case. The same one that's suing your old man and the entire State of New Mexico. And you, too, now that I think of it."

"I admire your gusto," Walker said. "You might even make an acceptable producer. You're certainly desperate and greedy enough. Of course, India will test you. India has been known to eat producers alive."

"Finish the script and I'll hire a rewrite man to switch it to Brazil."

"Now you're talking like a man I can trust," Walker said. "A man who can get the job done, no matter what the sacrifice."

"Look, Walker," A.D. said in an effort to nail down his intentions once and for all. "I've been on the road and I've sniffed up other people's exhaust. This is America. You're allowed to change horses in midstream. That's what the brochure says and that's what I'm going to do. You're my connection to some of that gold from the image bank, and I'm asking you: are you going to sign or not?"

"What's in it for me?"

"A way back into the action. You're out of touch, in case you haven't noticed. But I'm your transformer. That's a producer's job."

"How do you know I won't phone in the information to the old man and have done with it? I mean, all he's hanging in for is to find out about Clem."

"You won't do that. But if you do pull the plug on me, I'll break half the bones in your body. I'm playing hardball now, Walker. Forget dreamball."

"In that case, I'll sign," Walker said. He was enjoying A.D.'s intensity. "But if you're the producer you shouldn't get any more money from the old man. That's for the writer."

"That's not the way it works," said A.D., who had already lost more than half of the four thousand he had set aside for himself. "My money is supervising money. To see that you stay out of trouble and get the script done. Your old man knows that a man without product is only half a man. He wants to see you up on your feet and fully wrapped."

Walker signed the contract and put the ten grand in his pocket.

They drove the rest of the way in silence, arriving in Las Vegas for breakfast and checking into Caesar's Palace, a place they both knew too well. A.D. had played his share of gigs there in the past and Walker had wandered through on various lost weekends out of and away from Beverly Hills, mostly for championship fights and long bouts of compulsive fucking. After they had slept for a few hours, A.D. went off to the post office in the blazing sun to pick up the cashier's check from Wesley, and Walker went to the casino.

Walker played recklessly, without paying much attention to the cards, and lost over two thousand dollars in an hour. He didn't mind losing. In fact, more than a part of him was engaged in losing, and he played hundred-dollar chips without caution or design. It was 11 a.m. and there weren't many people around and the air had been pumped full of oxygen so that there was more than enough to go around. Despite the ionized air the blackjack dealers were more mechanical and bored than usual, and Walker changed tables a few times, either for luck or because he didn't like a dealer's vibrations. As he was about to leave and quit playing altogether, a woman sat down next to him. Her fingers were elegant and Oriental, with long tapering fingernails and an absence of rings. He guessed that she was Chinese. When he finally looked at her face she was more complicated than that. She was Eurasian, and her flat opaque eyes reflected only weariness and the distant possibility of play for pay. She wore a black silk dress with a high neck and the usual slit on the side. A delicate survey of wrinkles was visible on her upper neck and around her eyes. But it was her utter fatigue that comforted Walker, as when she checked him out while lighting a cigarette, her eyes staring blankly through him, bored and unseeing. He forgot about her while he won and then lost a few hundred dollars, but when she got up to leave he followed in her wake, sitting next to her at another table. After she lost, he shoved a pile of chips toward her. They played anonymously until the cocktail waitress came around and he bought her a brandy and soda.

"What do you have in mind?" She tapped on the table for a card replacement.

"I thought we might spend some time together."

As they got up to leave, a hand touched Walker's shoulder. The hand was large and well manicured and belonged to a tall, distinguished man in horn-rimmed glasses and gray sideburns. He was dressed in a white tennis outfit and carried two racquets. Next to him was a smaller, rotund man and a thin blond girl with a perfectly shaped Revlon face. They, too, wore white tennis outfits.

"Walker Hardin. My God." The man in the horn-rimmed glasses seemed genuinely shocked. "I thought you were in China or Korea or someplace."

Walker nodded, trying to place the man's face.

"Ben," the man said, picking up on Walker's disorientation. "Ben Copperthwaite. I was production manager on *The Last Charge*. You and your sister were in that scene on the river. Jesus, you must have been no more than eleven or twelve. An obnoxious brat. Remember? The boat tipped over. I'll never forget it. Your old man flipped out and fired a busload of people."

Walker didn't remember but he said he did and they chatted for a while, Ben introducing his tennis partners with names Walker immediately forgot and Walker mumbling a reference to the exhausted woman standing next to him as "one of my Eastern business partners."

"I have my own production company now." Ben's tight busy smile took in Walker's sneakers, bandaged leg, cut-off jeans, red cowboy shirt, and dark glasses, as well as the silver-tipped cane A.D. had bought him. "Three to five pictures a year, although I'll tell you, L.A. feels like Detroit in the thirties. Nothing moving. Absolutely nothing. All they want are these thirty-million-dollar cartoons or some jerk-off soap that can't get on without one of six stars who get two or three million guaranteed. It's obscene. No one pays anyone and no one makes decisions. But you know all that bullshit. Tell me, Walk, what are you up to?"

"I'm writing a script."

"It's in your blood, that's for sure. I'm still a big fan of your father's, you know. I've heard the stories, of course."

"He's in Mexico."

"Sensational," Ben said. "He can work for me anytime. Tell him I love him and that he's one of the real articles we have left in this rotten business. He's a professional, not one of these amateur bimbos I seem to have to deal with all the time." His eyes shifted to take in A.D. as he appeared by Walker's side, looking unexpectedly sartorial in gray Giorgio Armani slacks and a black Pierre Cardin shirt with bone-white buttons. All highlighted by his black eye patch.

"My producer," Walker said, making the introductions.

"You're working with a first-class talent," Ben said to A.D. "Join us in my suite and we'll celebrate."

Walker tried to beg off but A.D. was insistent and the Oriental woman whose name turned out to be Rosie didn't seem to mind one way or the other, and so they took the elevator up to Ben's suite, which was furnished with a piano, winding staircase, pink velvet couches, ceiling-to-floor columns, and a three-foot television screen.

"Now tell me about the project," Ben said as the portly man helped him slip into a maroon smoking jacket and went off to make a round of Bloody Marys.

"It's a love story that takes place in India," A.D. said, planting his feet on top of a glass coffee table. "A triangle between three Americans. Wesley is obsessed with it, especially as Walker is writing it. There is a lot of intensity between these two. I went down to New Mexico while he was shooting and talked to him about it, and it turns out that he's always been fascinated by the East. When Walker showed up having been over there, well, you know, it was a natural."

"I love it," Ben said. "It's like the Fondas or John and Walter Huston going off to make *The Treasure of the Sierra Madre*. And of course there are all those frozen rupees in India just waiting for American investors. It makes sense, financially, creatively, emotionally. You can live like a maharaja. I did a little film once in Bali. It was never released, but it was one of the most satisfying trips in my entire life."

"Peaches and cream," the blond girl said. "I'd love to go on a trip like that."

Ben patted her on the leg.

The portly man, who appeared to be some sort of assistant, went over a side table behind the TV screen and made a series of intense phone calls. The blond girl asked Rosie if she had ever heard of a certain skin lotion she was now using, and Rosie shrugged and said she didn't think so but that she had tried a lot of different lotions and she often found herself doing things and then not really remembering them.

"Seriously," Ben asked, "how is Wes? Everyone says he should check into the puzzle factory. I just hope it's not his health."

"The script has given him a second life," A.D. said. "He can't wait to get into the saddle again. You can't believe the ideas he comes up with."

"Money is hard these days," Ben said. "Especially if you're seventy years old and just fired off a film and your last three efforts have taken dives at the box office."

"The man's a legend in his own time," A.D. insisted.

"No question about that." Ben smiled at A.D. in a way that let him know he was under suspicion of being an amateur bimbo. "No doubt you have private financing already locked up. Hell, if Wesley pulled one off no one would applaud more than me. I trust you have a backup country if India doesn't pan out?"

"Mexico," A.D. said. "Or some place like that."

"If you switch locations south of the border, come and see me. And Walker, I'm interested in the script. Especially if Wesley decides it's time to write his memoirs. In fact, let's get together when you get back to town. Say at the end of the week."

Walker said he would get in touch and then asked Rosie if she was ready to leave.

"You're welcome here," A.D. said to her warmly.

She looked from one to the other, weighing her needs, and then stood up next to Walker, who shook hands with Ben and clapped A.D. on the shoulder, telling him how much faith he had in him as a producer. Then he and Rosie took the elevator down to his room.

Rosie kicked off her shoes and went straight to bed, sliding in between the sheets.

"Do you want me?" she asked.

"I think so," Walker said, sitting down on the edge of the bed.

She stared up at him with her hard weary eyes. "I might nod out on you if you don't get it on soon. I've been working too hard. I need a vacation."

"I haven't made it with anyone for a few years," he confessed.

"You must be a fag. Not that it makes any difference. I'm good with fags as long as they don't get too emotionally weird on me."

"It's not that. My wife died and I never got to it again."

"I'm the opposite," she said. "When someone dies on me, I can't get enough."

"I guess I've been shut down," he said.

"For two hundred dollars I'll take care of your fear for the rest of the day. I can't promise the night."

As he took off his clothes she noticed the bandage over his leg. "My producer shot me when I tried to run away," he explained.

"Film scum," she said, as if she knew what she was talking about.

He lay down on the bed but refrained from touching her. Staring at the ceiling, he said: "There's a line in *The African Queen* when Humphrey Bogart and Katharine Hepburn are floating down this river and he says to her: 'Pinch me, Rosie. Here we are, going down the river like Anthony and Cleopatra.'"

"Do you feel we're floating down a river?" she asked as her fingers reached over and caressed his cock.

"In a way."

"Then why don't you slide inside me so that you can get with the current."

Turning her over on her side, he entered into her. Holding her breasts and shutting his eyes, he remained very still, breathing evenly and smelling the faint perfume in her hair. When she finally responded, sighing and moving her hips, he stopped her, his hand pressing down on her thigh. They remained that way for several minutes, not moving, his breathing matching hers. His mind empty, he felt his blood roaring through him and a delicious agony invading his entire body. He passed through that and entered a quiet place, a calm that was soon replaced by fear as she started to move again and he felt he was going to explode, but she pulled herself in and the pressure in his throat and ears receded as she lay perfectly still. He had no idea who she was and in fact had no memory of her, even the color of her hair. She might have been asleep except that she was saying, "You're on the money, honey. Hold it right there." He held it right there while a great shaking sadness stole into him that began in his feet and swept up into his loins, and on the crest of that terrifying emptiness, he came.

Rosie immediately fell asleep while Walker lay awake and thought of his wife for the first time since her death and the last time they had made love when she had been so freaked and lustful lying underneath him on the sandy soil somewhere in the middle of the scorched plains of India. Some clinging residue of the smell and taste of her enveloped him for a moment, and to stop thinking about her, he went over to the desk and began to write.

DELHI. TRAIN STATION — MIDDAY... *Jim and Lacey descend from the train carrying only one bag apiece. Stunned and dazed from the blistering heat, they walk slowly down the crowded platform.... A plump Indian in a white shirt and pale blue turban stands at the end of the platform with a sign:* Jim and Lacey Rankin...*"You are to please follow me," he says, picking up their bags as they identify themselves. They follow him through the station and onto the street to an old white Chrysler sedan parked in back of a ricksha stand. The driver puts their bags in the trunk and opens the back door.... A blond, blue-eyed woman, large-boned and fleshy underneath a straw hat and yellow cotton dress, leans over from the backseat, one leg extended in a plaster cast. "Must excuse me," she says in a high-pitched upper-class English accent. "Broke my foot falling off a horse. Humiliating. I'm Miranda Witherspoon. So glad. Terrible time. Not sure what train you were on, your telegram from Madras very vague. Your father called this morning all lathered up about your missing sister. Your father is a lion to work for. My husband, Charles, is quite ter-*

rified of him. I say, you're traveling awfully light.". . . Lacey explains that the rest of their bags were stolen on the train. . . . Miranda is outraged. "How ugly it's all getting. There's no point in traveling any more. It's a defensive life now, at best. . . . But never mind. Everything can be replaced and it's more amusing to have your clothes made for you here. One never brings the right things.". . . The huge car slowly maneuvers through a side street as hands press against the window for alms. They turn into a wide boulevard, passing government buildings and then a row of fashionable hotels and villas set back from the road. Entering through an open iron gate, they park in front of a large nineteenth-century colonial house surrounded by flat well-clipped lawns and a variety of terraced flower gardens. Suddenly they are harbored inside a familiar world of comfort and control and they are glad to be there. . . . A uniformed servant opens the door and they follow Miranda as she hobbles inside. . . .

TO THE INTERIOR . . . Charles Witherspoon, his taut athletic face full of concern and studied alertness, strides across the cool Cambodian tiles of the veranda, through the narrow glass doors, into the spacious Edwardian living room where they all stand waiting for him, servants offering glasses of sherry and elegant hors d'oeuvres. Charles wears white cotton slacks and a starched white shirt with pink collar and is all business and hysterical prep-school charm. . . . "Wonderful to finally see you. I'll fill you in on your sister before your father's call. That's in a few hours. I've quite a sheet on her, but you'll be relieved to know she's okay. Just off on various pilgrimages here and there. Religious trips, mostly. A common enough ailment in this country. Right now she's off in Benares or thereabouts, questing or seeking, I suppose you would say. But God, you probably want to change and have a bath before we get into all of that.". . .

INTERIOR . . . Their suite of rooms is modern and air-conditioned and looks out on the gardens and a flock of wandering peacocks. . . . "So that's it," Jim says, after they have each bathed and Jim is changing into his pants. "We'll get drunk tonight and go back in the morning.". . . Lacey has changed into a blue sari that Miranda has loaned her and looks odd and strangely childlike. "I don't see why we should go back. We've already put a lot into finding her. We've been drugged and robbed and molested, *for god's sake. Although once I knew they weren't going to kill or rape us I leaned into it a little.".…"What do you mean, leaned into it?".…"Some part of me was stimulated.".… He looks at her as if she's lost her mind. "Listen, Lacey, I'm not in good shape and I want to go home. My sister doesn't need us. It's obvious that she doesn't want to be found. She's never had the consideration to even send anyone a postcard. She's been totally self-indulgent and I don't see why I have to waste my life trying to find her, especially now that she's off on a lark with some guru.".…"Aren't you curious?" Lacey asks.…"Not really.".… But Lacey persists: "If you don't have the energy to find her, how do you expect me to find you or you to find me?".… The question infuriates him: "Sweet Jesus. I can't stand that kind of talk. I don't want to find you. You don't want to find me. In any case we're right in front of each other.".…"Then maybe I should step off to the side, away from you, because I have no idea who I am around you." … "Maybe you should," he says, pulling back within himself.…*

INTERIOR… *On that edge they descend to the garden, where Charles meets them inside a cool marble gazebo on the far side of the lawn. Jim asks after his father.…"He has called off the search for your sister," Charles replies with a weary smile. "I spoke to him two days ago. Apparently she has written him a letter. He wouldn't disclose the contents, but one must assume she's well. He's anxious to talk to you, of course." He opens a large notebook bound in brown leather. "Let me start from that point where your sister left Madras, which is where your knowledge of her ends. She flew to Delhi and spent two and a half weeks at the Imperial Hotel. From there she took the train to Jaipur, where she stayed for over a month, keeping to herself and seeing no one. She took her meals in her room and every afternoon walked in the gardens of the hotel, which once belonged to a maharaja and which is all very grand. Four months later she turned up in Poona to study with Sri Iynagar, a renowned yoga teacher with an international reputation. Perhaps you know of him? Aside from regularly attending yoga classes, she underwent rigorous purification asanas, which involved fasting for a month and cleaning out her entire intestinal tract. After several months studying with Iynagar she met a French disciple of Bhagwan Sri Raj Neesh, a most radical and* controversial teacher who was at that time living in Poona. Your sister and the Frenchman became lovers and she moved into his rented room in a large house near the ashram inhabited by other sannyasins. They listened to Bhagwan's daily lectures and participated in several training courses or intensives on various meditation techniques, modern as well as traditional, such as primal therapy and vipassana. But your sister was never able to become a disciple of Bhagwan. Even though she wore orange, the prescribed color at the ashram, she refused to wear the mala over her neck with Bhagwan's picture hanging from it. She and the Frenchman quarreled. He insisted that she surrender to Raj Neesh and she grew more stubborn in her refusals. Finally she left altogether and hired a car to take her to Bombay. She rented a suite of rooms in the Taj Mahal Hotel and made contact with Western students living in cheap hotels nearby who supplied her with opium and hashish. During this time she made two visits to Ganeshpuri to visit Swami Mucktananda's ashram, a day's drive from Bombay. Three months later she appears in Goa living with an American in a small house on the beach. He is known to the rather bizarre and anachronistic collection of Westerners living there as Jack the Smack, with a reputation for having supported himself exporting jewelry and religious objects to the West, mostly through smuggling. But I gathered that he and your sister were at first obsessively in love and never out of each other's sight. But then she began to withdraw into herself, meditating or taking long aimless walks down the beach. Once she sat outside the house for a day and a half without moving and refused all efforts to communicate. Jack the Smack tried to ignore her and involved himself in the soft traffic of Goa hustles and pleasures. But one night her relentless self-absorption enraged him and he lost control, knocking her across the room where she fell against a chair and badly bruised her shoulder. They never spoke again and the next day she left. Two months later she showed up outside of New Delhi to attend a meditation camp run by a Burmese Buddhist monk. She had acute dysentery and the camp was very rough and primitive with fourteen hours of sitting meditation a day. But she survived, afterwards returning to Delhi and leaving immediately for Dharamsala in the north to visit a Tibetan refugee camp.

While there, she took refuge with a Lama Yeshe and after studying with him for six months left for the Kulu valley in the foothills of the Himalayas, intending to do a year's retreat. At first she lived in a cave, but was unable to adjust to the brutal conditions and moved to a small house, outside of a small town, with no heat or plumbing. After several weeks her health deteriorated, and she returned to Delhi to consult a doctor as well as Lama Yeshe, who had moved there with his family. I spoke to him a few days ago. Your sister stayed in Delhi for several months, and when she regained her health she went on a pilgrimage to Saranath, hoping to complete her prostrations. She is most likely there now.". . . Charles looks up from his notebook, snapping it shut and pouring them martinis from a portable bar. "That sort of thing happens over here," Charles says. "Exotic obsessions of deliverance which leave the mind strung out on deluded hope and the stomach full of parasites.". . .

(Dear Pop. I'm stopping here for a beat. The stench of too much exposition, for one thing. But that phone call is similar to the one we had when I called you from Benares. Do you remember? You were shooting that feeble comedy in the south of France. I hung up when you started screaming at me to come home, that as far as you were concerned it was okay if you never saw Clem again. She had made her decision to disappear and you had made your decision to let her. I have many of those same feelings about you these days, Pop. . . . As for now, I'm sitting in room 703 in Caesar's Palace planning to drive to Albany and see Lama Yeshe, who, if he is there, will most likely know if Clem is still on the planet. Room 703 reminds me of *Bustin' Out*, which you started in Vegas in September of '73 and didn't finish until March of '74. You fired me twice on that one before I quit altogether. But as one of three associate producers, I managed to scam twenty-five grand off the top with the help of the prop man and the production manager. Old Teddy Penders and Benson. Part of your family. Over fifteen pictures together. They stole you blind, and not only that, they didn't have much respect for you. Benson said you hadn't done any good work since the late fifties. Certainly *Bustin' Out* proves that theory. Your moves on that one were so off the wall that it gave me the courage to try and separate myself from you altogether. But it wasn't until I went off to India that I made any headway on that score. What a drag it was then and still is to talk to you, as if you swallowed whole all that public relations baloney about being one of the few people in the business who have any real compassion or moral code. All that hype about you being a frontier man, aligned in the pantheon with Ford, Raoul Walsh, and Hawks, just crafting your entertainments for the general populace. Maybe so. But I'm aware of how numb and antagonistic you are to everything outside of your immediate desires, except, of course, your "work," which you pull around you like a slimy second skin so that you won't have to live or be responsible for the other layers of your life.)

Back to the script, which brings us to the phone call and Jim picking up the phone in Charles's study with its huge portrait of Kipling staring down from over the mantel. "Hello, hello," he yells into the receiver. "Pop?"…"Yes, yes," thunders old Pete. "I received a letter from your sister last week that has me just about buffaloed. I'm calling off the hunt. I think she's gone over the edge. Some kind of one-year meditation retreat in Nepal or some godforsaken place. Going on about a guru or a teacher and how happy she is and how good and accepting she feels about me. I don't trust any of it. In fact I find it embarrassing. I immediately sent her a telegram informing her that when she got her head clear I'd be glad to see her but not before. Do you hear me? I'm fed up with the whole goddamned performance and I don't want you dealing with it any more. Are they treating you well over there? They sound like rank amateurs to me. Especially what's his name? Charles. In fact, I don't think the corporation should continue dealing with that part of the world. They're falling behind too fast. It's not practical to rescue those parts of the third world that are threatening to become the fourth and even the fifth world."…"I want to find her," Jim says. "She's been sick."..."That's up to you," roars Pete. "But I would prefer that you and Lacey take a two-week vacation in Bali or Australia or wherever you want and then come home by way of Hong Kong. There's a firm I'm thinking of absorbing and I'd like you to check it out."..."Pop. Perhaps you didn't hear. I'm not going to do any of that right now."..."I assume you're coming back to work. You have a lot of responsibilities back here."..."I'm not coming back until I find Clem," Jim says, surprised at what he is saying. "In fact, as of now I'm quitting."... There is a long silence before old Pete says in a flat, controlled voice: "So be it," and hangs up.... Jim puts the phone softly back on its cradle and says to Lacey, who has come into the room: "I'm going to have to look for a job."... Lacey puts her arms around him, kisses him. "Good. I'll look for one too."...

EXTERIOR—NIGHT... Charles drives them to the edge of old Delhi, where they leave him sitting behind the wheel. They walk into the smoky evening light, past wandering sacred cows, fried pancake stands, tinkling rickshas and bicycles, beggars mumbling for annas in front of cloth merchants hawking cheap paisley spreads. They stop outside a four-story wooden building with a rickety staircase winding up the outside. Jim asks a toothless hag if she knows where the Tibetan lives. She shakes her head, not understanding. "Lama! Lama!" Jim shouts and finally she nods, laughing and pointing to the roof. They climb the stairs to the roof where Lama Yeshe sits on a simple cane chair, a dozen or more people seated cross-legged in front of him. They are in the middle of a puja and Lama Yeshe's eyes are half closed, his right hand slowly moving a dorje in loose circular motions while his left hand rings a bell. He is a thin brown man of indeterminate age with an enormous shaved head and sad liquid eyes. His young wife sits in front of him in a black chuba, playing with their two small children as the puja proceeds. The others are all Tibetans except for a blond bearded man sitting off to one side, slowly shifting the wooden beads of his mala between thumb and forefinger as he intones the solemn requests and prayers dedicated to the wrathful deity, Dorje Phourba.

Walker stopped writing and laid his head over his folded arms, sleeping for a few moments before he moved to the bed and curled up beside Rosie. Several hours later, when A.D. came back to the room, Walker was huddled in the same position. A.D. read the pages on the table and, in a move that was becoming automatic, went down to the casino's office to have them Xeroxed. When he returned, Rosie was in the shower and Walker was sitting up in bed, drinking coffee and eating a sweet roll.

"I'm going to Albany," Walker said.

"Say what?" A.D. sat on the edge of the bed and drank some of Walker's coffee.

"I've come to that point in the script where I have to find out about Clementine."

"You mean if she's dead or not?"

"Something like that."

"Why? The script can take off on its own. If you need her to be dead, make her dead."

"I'm ready to go outside the script," Walker said simply.

Rosie came out of the shower wrapped in a towel. Abruptly she took the coffee cup out of A.D.'s hands and went over to sit on the other bed, as if protecting her right to food and privacy.

"I'll head for New York," A.D. said. "It's time to ram a deal through the money people."

"What money people?"

"Whoever's hanging around."

"There won't be anyone hanging around. The old man's recent actions don't exactly inspire that kind of attention."

"Fuck your old man," A.D. said. "We agreed on that, didn't we? I'm just worried about the product. If you find out too much about your sister, you might not want to continue. You might not have the need."

"That's possible," Walker said.

Rosie slowly finished her coffee and let the towel covering her waist slide to the floor. "If someone wants to take a turn with me, that's okay. If not I'm going to mingle with the high rollers."

"I'll take you on," A.D. said with a sigh.

An hour later he was still negotiating when Walker, suitcase in hand, waved good-bye and left.

THE NEXT day A.D. flew to New York. He was coming off the road missing one eye and just as broke as when he left. All he had going for him was a long-shot movie hustle dependent on a used-up director just fired off his last picture who thought he was dying or wanted to die or was afraid to die. Not to mention the director's son, the Far East man, who held the keys to the story line and was another kind of casualty altogether. And then, of course, there was India, which A.D. refused to think about.

When he arrived at Kennedy Airport he checked into the airport bar for courage. Three drinks later he felt as if all the weary little dues and leaks in confidence and energy he had accumulated over the past month had suddenly surfaced and were demanding to be accounted for. His body ached as if it had been kicked, and his entire respiratory system seemed filled with a threat of foreclosure. He was holding himself so maniacally on the point that he had forgotten how to crawl off to the side and check for missing parts. In the face of all this he told himself that even if he was riding the wrong horse, it was the only horse he had and he was committed to flogging it until it crossed the finish line or dropped. Unfortunately he had forgotten to arrange for a place to stay and was unable to reach anyone on the phone. His lack of funds made him settle on the George Washington Hotel, one step away from the street and a step he had made too many times, down to and up from. Lying naked in the hot dead air of his room, he listened to the traffic outside and thought of Wesley Hardin making air-conditioned deals at the Sherry Netherland. Even though it was close to midnight he decided to call him anyway.

Evelyn answered the phone.

"I'd like to turn in a few pages and pick up some cash," he said.

"I guess so," she replied vaguely, not sure whom she was talking to.

A.D. tried to make the connection for her. "When you held my hand that time in the hospital it got me through a rough patch."

She remembered and said she would see him when he got there.

But instead of going directly to the Sherry Netherland, A.D. walked down Third Avenue, then across St. Mark's Place to Second Avenue, and down Second to a small nightclub, the Blue Rooster. Over the years A.D. had booked several acts into the Rooster and often used the place as a hangout. He had on his Vegas wardrobe, light maroon slacks and a lemon-colored shirt plus a Samsonite briefcase. His change in style, together with his black eye patch, caused the bartender to drop behind the bar in feigned astonishment.

"Mr. Ballou," he said on reappearing. "You've made a score."

"I have at that," A.D. admitted. "More or less."

One of the semiregulars, a black bass player, approached him from the men's room. "A.D., my main man," he exclaimed with exaggerated warmth. "You're lookin' good, *real* good. Can you lend me a deuce?"

A.D. gave him a fifth of what he asked for and after a few mumbled words about the futility of life in general the bass player slipped out the door to "see a man about a Chinese lady."

A.D. went over to the piano and bunched a few chords together. He felt disoriented and melancholy and unable to repress the doubts gnawing up inside him.

The owner of the club, a fat middle-aged Italian in a stained sweat shirt and baggy tuxedo pants, leaned over the back of the piano.

"Sorry about the eye," he said in a flat voice. "But the patch does something for you. You must have lost it on the road."

"More or less on the road," A.D. said, not wanting to get into it. "I've got a lawsuit going."

"Litigation is good for the soul," the owner said. "As long as you don't count on a payoff. I've got several going myself. By the way, I'm looking for a manager for this joint."

"I've changed my game," A.D. said. "I'm into films. You ever hear of Wesley Hardin? I'm producing something for him."

"Didn't he do a Western with Clint Eastwood?"

"Probably. He's cornered the market on Westerns."

"I heard they aren't making them any more."

"I'm pushing him into a new genre. High adventure set in India."

"Why not?" the owner said, not believing him. "When you strike out in Hollywood, get back to me. Once a nickel-and-dime man always a nickel-and-dime man. I think Cagney said that."

A.D. pushed back the piano stool. "I'll send you a ticket to the first screening."

He made his way into the thick humid night wishing he was anywhere else but New York. As he walked slowly uptown, he tried to find a rhythm or attitude that would let him sting and float with Wesley, but when he arrived at the Sherry Netherland he was tight and breathless and decidedly off the point.

When Wesley opened the door, he barely glanced at A.D.; his attention was nailed to the scene behind him where Sidney, the second unit cameraman, Evelyn, and a distraught bald-headed man in a blue and white seersucker suit peered anxiously out an open window. An older couple in evening clothes sat on the couch, refusing to acknowledge Wesley pacing back and forth.

"There's been an accident," the man said. A.D. recognized him as an English character actor, a colonel or a butler or a chauffeur.

"Not at all," replied the white-haired woman sitting next to him. "It was quite deliberate. Wesley threw it through the window with both hands. If anyone is killed, he'll go to jail and I won't raise one finger in his defense." She twisted her thin patrician head to stare up at A.D. "Are you the house detective? If so, I suggest an action."

"I'm a producer."

"Indeed. Then you are useless."

Wesley came to a halt in front of her. He looked quite mad standing there in his silk pajama bottoms and loose karate jacket, his thick white hair sticking straight out from the sides of his head as if an electric current had run through it. A.D. was stunned at how pale and thin he was and it occurred to him that Wesley was incapable of directing a film, not to mention his own life.

"Amanda, my darling," Wesley said, looking down on her. "You are a ferocious and ignorant cunt."

"And you have lost your mind," she replied. "You haven't had anything new to say for years. I can't even remember when you last directed a decent picture, let alone a semicoherent scene. You've lost your dignity, and it's shameful, Wesley."

"Here, here," her companion said stiffly. "I must say, Wesley, as much as we have been devoted to you in the past, it seems impossible to continue being a witness to your willful disintegration."

"Then I suggest you leave."

"Our intention exactly."

As they stood up there was a knock on the door.

"I'll handle this one," the bald-headed man said. "It will be my last act as your agent."

He opened the door to let in the hotel manager.

"Has there been loss of life?" Amanda asked.

"No one was hurt, thank God," said the manager. "But I must ask you to remain until this is sorted out. I don't want to have to call the police."

Amanda pushed him out of the way. "Don't be absurd. Mr. Hardin is solely responsible for this act, as he is for all his acts."

As Evelyn and Wesley moved forward with the agent to deal with the hotel manager, Sidney motioned to A.D. to join him in the bedroom.

"He threw my video camera out the window," Sidney said, closing the door and sitting down on the bed. "I can't be in that room any more. I'm trying to keep it contained, but when the surf is up with Wes it's hard to stay in the water. And it was very good what he was doing. He was actually weeping at one point, talking about his friends that had died, different films, that whole scandal with Jack Warner and Errol Flynn. And then he just says this is totally profane and that he hates video, the way it gets under the skin and promotes the wrong kind of information, how falsely seductive it is. He started to rant on and on and I said, hey, listen, you were the one that asked for video. Most of the stuff I shot is in sixteen. I don't care about video. Let's never mention the word again. And he says 'right' and throws the fucking thing out the window."

He paused, realizing that A.D. didn't know who he was.

"I was second unit with Wesley in Durango when he lost it. He asked me to shoot all this crazy stuff and I did and I've just kept going. I developed some footage in L.A. and came here to shoot more. You're A.D., right? The doctor or shrink who's taking care of Walker."

"I've been working with Walker on a script, if that's what you mean. I'm the producer."

"Right. I knew someone was working with him. Wesley told

me he was trying to promote this script as a catharsis for him or something."

"It's a good script," A.D. said. "I think it's hot."

Sidney walked to the bed and then to the window and back to the bed again. Picking up an ashtray, he put it back on the dresser, then lit a cigarette and stabbed it out on a paperback book. Finally he came to rest full length on the bed. Staring up at the ceiling, he said:

"I looked at the script. Tell you the truth, I don't know what kind of a pull it has. I mean, who cares about India? Indiana maybe, but not India. I'll tell you another thing. No one wants to go there. I wouldn't go. I have enough problems. Everyone will get sick and freak out, and it'll be a producer's nightmare. Wesley won't last one week down there. Count on it. I was with him in Mexico. But rain or shine, the old bastard is still trying to get into gear, setting up meetings and leaking all kinds of malarkey to the press. He thinks that if he isn't riding herd on a project, he's going to cash in."

"Is he?"

"I'm certainly banking on it."

"Doesn't he want to know about his daughter?"

"Not really. That's wrap-up stuff. What you do when you have no time left. It's automatic. Mostly the kids are a pain in the ass. I know this tale you and Walker are laying out has put him through changes."

"I have more pages for him."

"Then he'll go through more changes."

"What about his wife? Doesn't she stroke him down?"

"She's holding on, but it's hard. He accuses her of waiting for him to die and they fight and she disappears for a day or two and he totally loses control."

A.D. went into the bathroom and splashed cold water on his face. He checked the medicine cabinet. There was an impressive display of mood elevators and painkillers, and he put a few of each into his pocket.

"Are you making a film about Wesley?" A.D. asked, coming back into the room.

"I am, but not like the family soap you're doing. I'm traveling the low road, catching what dribbles out of the mouth after the main meal is over. Final words and that kind of thing. I pile up moments, vicious little scenes, tearful, angry, guilty, they're all the same to me as long as they add up to some kind of confession. That's where the gold is."

"What kind of a deal do you have with Wesley?"

Sidney sat up on the bed and looked straight at A.D. as if he wanted to impress him with his intentions.

"No deal."

"You mean he's not paying you?"

"I don't want him to. That way I own the stock. I never cashed the checks he sent me."

"Does he know that?"

"I don't think so. I sent him a memo which he never looked at and which I Xeroxed, so I'm covered."

"Can you afford to keep going?"

"Probably not."

"And you think this can make money?"

"Are you kidding? There's only one law in this business and that's box office. I'm doing my best to obey that law. There's nobody over me and no middle man and it doesn't cost anything to shoot. I've got Evelyn stripped to the bone screaming how she loves and hates him and I show how she gets him up in the morning, convincing him that he has something to live for. I've got fights and harangues and secrets revealed. I have this one scene in Mazatlán where he throws a knife at some L.A. lawyer and it sticks in his arm. And Wesley's in the news, you know. He's all over the place. Everyone has an opinion on him."

From that moment on, India was never a serious issue for A.D.

"There should be a way to put everything on the same plate," he said to Sidney, who had gone over to the door and was trying to listen to what was being said in the other room. "I'll give you a slice of India if you cut me into your action with Wesley."

"I don't need India," Sidney said. "I need fifty grand. If not from you, then from somebody."

"We'll talk about it," A.D. said, noticing that Sidney had lost most of his initial authority and that the mention of money made his body contract. "Where are you staying?"

"Downtown."

"I'll call you when I find a place to stay. I'm at the Hilton and I can't stand it. The service is lousy and there are too many tourists."

"I have an extra room. Wesley likes to come down to hide out. Maybe it would make it easier for you."

"I'll be there tomorrow."

Sidney stepped away from the door and wrote his address on a piece of paper in large bold letters. "I'll give you the bottom line," he said wearily. "I can't stand the abuse. Like this thing with the video camera. He's got me so twisted. It's not like he doesn't know what he's doing. He knows exactly where the lens is. But he keeps pulling the rug out from under himself. Every time he quits he asks me back, and then he quits again."

He opened the door and A.D. followed him into the other room.

Wesley was sitting with Evelyn on the couch. Everyone else had gone. Whatever had gone down with the agent and hotel manager, it had left them in a different mood and they seemed more relaxed, even somewhat animated. Wesley got up and spread his arms, including them in a sudden benediction.

"Every time I shake the goddamned tree and more rotten apples fall out, I think, that's it, I'm free, and even though I know there are always more, I'm grateful these particular ones are on the ground."

"Amen," Evelyn said.

She had curled into the corner of the couch and was looking up at Wesley with great wariness as he put an arm around Sidney and kissed him on the cheek, talking loudly into his ear.

"Your video camera sliced straight through the awning and almost took a guy's head off. Turns out that one of my pictures, *Wishbone*, is in his all-time top-five pantheon, and he refuses to make a complaint. All he wants is an autographed copy of the script. Funny, I can't even remember who wrote it. But I don't take anything back about the video machine. I hate it. Let's never mention it again. I tell you what, though, you and me, Sidney, we have to keep shooting. That's all we're good for, peering through the lens. But now we'll mix in some scenes from Walker's script. What do you think, A.D.?"

"You're the boss," A.D. said, trying to make whatever switch was called for.

A.D. had not fully recovered from the shock of seeing Wesley and Evelyn for the first time, having been blind, of course, back in New Mexico. He had imagined Wesley six inches taller and a hundred pounds heavier, not this frail and precarious old man who was so obviously on the drift. And he felt unnerved and totally unprepared for Evelyn, with her absence of show business persona, the almost lethal way she sat within her own silence, how physically strong and elastic her body seemed inside her black jeans and simple white T-shirt.

Wesley sat down on the couch and lifted one of Evelyn's bare feet to kiss. "I want to get moving on India, bring all of that together. It might be time to pull the plug on this screwed-up country and sign up for a location trip. That's always the best part, when you're just looking and not trying to force it all into some mediocre story line."

He paused, staring off across the room, then back again to A.D. "Where's Walker?" he asked, with sudden alarm.

"He's driving from Vegas to Albany. He said it was time to find out if Clementine was still alive. I guess there's somebody there who knows."

"She's alive," Wesley said flatly. "The script demands it."

A.D. took the new pages out of his briefcase and handed them to Wesley.

"And how is Walker?" Wesley asked, uneasily flipping through the pages. "Has he managed to find any kind of reality for himself?"

"I don't know about reality," A.D. said. "But he's nailed to the script, and that keeps him straight. He doesn't say much and he hangs out by himself. Of course I've been watching out for him, seeing that he doesn't graze off or get into trouble, and that's been a full-time job. I'm here to tell you that. He's more sideways than streetwise, you understand, so I've had to keep him on a short leash. I busted his ass a few times to make sure the pages got squeezed out and I fixed up a few scenes, gave them a wash and a rinse. I guess you know that he's not a natural-born writer, but when the mood is on him he can burn. Other than that, my main problem is living with the one eye."

A.D. paused and went over to the other couch and sat down next to Sidney, who had made himself a tall brandy and soda and wasn't listening to any of it. "It hasn't been easy," A.D. said slowly. "Some actions won't never be the same."

"The patch works real well," Wesley said, bragging on him. "I'd cast you as a heavy anytime."

"You already did," A.D. said. "Which reminds me, I'll need some scratch for those new pages and for those times I helped Walker out in Vegas."

"Was it roulette?" Wesley asked.

"Mostly blackjack. One bad run."

"Drugs?"

"Just maintenance and travel aids."

"Women?"

"I set him up a time or two."

"I'm grateful," Wesley said, with what looked like tears in his eyes. "Would a few grand do you?"

"For now. Of course the game has changed a little and I'm sure you'll appreciate that. I'm one of the producers now. Walker and I signed a paper to that effect, and if you sign that'll make it official."

"I don't care who the producer is," Wesley said, signing the paper A.D. offered him. "We'll need more than one producer before we're through. But this is the core group. This is it. After all these years this is the gang I finish up with."

Sidney drained his brandy and soda. "What about me? I don't want to finish up with you but I wouldn't mind making a deal."

"You're my trigger man," Wesley said impatiently. "Without you I don't see."

Evelyn uncurled herself from the couch, looking bored and weary. "I'm going to get some air, if there is any out there."

Wesley sprang to his feet. "We'll go over to the Russian Tea Room for borscht and a few drinks."

They took the elevator down to the lobby and entered into the dense August night. In his pale blue pajama pants and karate jacket Wesley looked like an old martial arts freak who had wandered in from the park.

Wesley had trouble breathing and they sat down on a bench, their backs to the park, watching the street and the soft parade of people floating in and out of the Plaza and the movie house next door.

"I can't believe Clementine has really disappeared," Wesley said abruptly, his lungs struggling for air. "I can't grasp that. I was angry. Sure. She gives you no warning. But I certainly wasn't totally rejecting."

Evelyn looked at him with alarm and started to rub the back of his neck but he shook her off.

"Okay. I know," he said. "I won't get stuck back there. What's important is that we all get into the same room again."

He paused, staring back into the dark and silent park.

Sidney chose that moment to stand up and state his case to Wesley, something he had never done before. His pants and short-sleeved shirt were matted with sweat, and as he talked he pulled nervously at the tired flesh around his neck. "One minute you tell me I'm working for you and it's good steady work and don't worry, just pull the trigger. Then you don't pay me and when I say, okay, it's my film, you say, hey, we'll find the form, don't get attached. And now you pull me into an Indian project with your looney-tunes son and say, 'Just stay in the moment, baby.' I need *form*, Wesley. I'm an A to B man. Always have been, always will be. I don't mind playing and picking up spontaneous stuff, but pay me and give me an overall plan. And don't keep telling me it's my film or our film or your film or it's not a film but a 'probe into the unknown.' You're messing with my mind. And then to top it all off, A.D. starts pitching me about joining forces with him and making an end run on you. It's no good, Wesley. You've got to give me a real target and you've got to be straight with me."

"You're absolutely right," Wesley said.

This agreement took Sidney by surprise, and he stepped into and out of the park before he spoke to Wesley again. "Call me when you know what you want," he said. Then he crossed the street and walked across the square in front of the Plaza and disappeared down Fifth Avenue.

"Don't worry about Sidney," Wesley said. "He gets this way. Everyone does in this business. I'll make a deal with him and he'll quiet down. The truth is, he has a great pair of eyes and can enter into a space better than anyone I know. And it's my pleasure to exploit myself right now. I need to do that."

"Why?" Evelyn asked. "Why do you need to do that?"

Wesley looked at her a long time before he answered. "I have to hold on. If I don't hold on, I'll fall off. If I fall off, I'm lost forever."

"Lost and gone forever," Evelyn sang, leaning over and kissing him. "Dreadful sorry, Clementine."

WESLEY stood up and, with Evelyn and A.D. flanking him, walked alongside the park to Seventh Avenue and then south to Fifty-seventh Street. The Russian Tea Room was crowded, and Wesley pushed his way past the bar to the dining room. The maître d' failed to recognize him and bluntly refused him a table. As Wesley started to protest, his hand pulling vaguely at the maître d's lapel, a youthful figure in starched jeans and custom-made white Jamaica leisure shirt bounded toward him from a rear table.

"Oh, Christ," Evelyn muttered, unable to make an exit because of the steady crush of people pushing up behind her.

"Mr. Hardin. My God!" The youthful figure brushed past the maitre d' and claimed Wesley's arm. "How propitious. We were just talking about you. The way you've handled the press the past few weeks has been extraordinary."

"Do I know you?"

"Of course. It's just that all of us young moguls look alike these days. Bud Serkin."

"Warners?"

"Universal."

"On the way in or on the way out?"

"Hopefully sliding into the middle. Please, Mr. Hardin, you must join us. There's an old admirer of yours back there who will absolutely kill me if I let you slip away."

They followed Bud Serkin to his table, squeezing in around a handsome gray-haired woman and a delicately featured young man in lightly tinted dark glasses and a blue business suit whose thick blond hair was swept back from his forehead in a Rod Stewart brush.

"Long time no see," the woman said to Wesley.

"Hello, Sheila," Wesley said. "I thought you were dead."

"Just buried alive."

"It was always hard to tell with you."

"Indeed." She turned her hard gray eyes on Evelyn. "Aren't you going to introduce me to your new wife? Or is this your daughter?"

"Evelyn," Wesley said. "Sheila someone or other. An old associate of mine."

"You'll never forgive me for that lawsuit, will you?" Sheila asked.

"I never mind lawsuits," Wesley said. "Even between friends. It's who you have been revealed to be that's unforgivable."

"That's true," A.D. interjected, trying to get into the flow. "I'm suing him myself."

"There you go," Wesley said. "And this man is my producer."

"I heard you had another project launched," Bud Serkin said. "I must congratulate you on that. India or someplace, isn't it?"

"India. My son is scripting it."

"We have about twenty million in frozen rupees over there. I wish we could arrange for you to spend some of it for the studio, but with all the litigation surrounding you these days that's clearly impossible."

"We'll set up a meeting anyway," Sheila said. "You never know when one meeting might mutate into another, thus a project is born. Henry will see to it, won't you, dear?"

She patted the blond young man on the cheek. He nodded and made a note on a slip of paper with a gold-tipped pen.

"No meeting," Bud Serkin said. "But a dinner would be lovely. It's time for some sort of retrospective for Wesley. A testimonial. Hawks and Hitchcock had one. I even think old Sam Fuller must have had one."

Sheila finished patting the young man's cheek and smiled at Wesley. "Then you, too, will be buried alive."

Wesley nodded, not bothering to reply. He felt himself being pulled away as if he were floating above them, looking down on himself as well. From a distance he became aware of their words but was unable to distinguish any separate meanings so that the language flowed together into one sound, joining the larger sound of the room. He had the thought that he was wheeling above them for a crane shot, and he found it funny that the actors should be so out of control beneath him. He tried to form the words "who's directing?" but the words wouldn't form or they weren't hearing him. "Wesley, Wesley," it was Evelyn's voice, reaching out to him. But it was too late.

"For god's sake, why do you let him go out in this shape?" Wesley dimly heard Sheila ask Evelyn. "He's on his last legs."

"He does what he wants to do," Evelyn said matter-of-factly.

"Oh, rubbish. You can't just let him get drunk and pass out on the table like some kind of degenerate."

Evelyn stared hard at Sheila, so that Sheila had to lift up her glass and look away. "It's not that I give a damn," Sheila said. "It's just that it's distasteful and unnecessary."

"I agree," Wesley said thickly. "If you want a deal talk to my producer over here."

"I'm not making a deal with anyone," A.D. said. "Not even myself." He helped Wesley out of his chair and all three of them made their way back through the crowd and onto the street.

They walked toward Seventh Avenue until Wesley became dizzy again and sat down on the steps of Carnegie Hall. To one side a blind violinist in a New York Yankees cap played the Bach Chaconne.

"Are you in pain?" Evelyn asked.

"Not hardly," Wesley replied. As if to prove his point he stood up and tapped the violinist on the shoulder. Handing him a wad of bills, he took up the violin and started to play, the bow scratching over the strings as he sang in a hoarse baritone:

> "'Twas on the tenth of March, my friend,
>   As you may understand.
>   Two men from Labrador
>   Started for Newfoundland.
>   'Twas eight o'clock in the morning
>   As they left Point Amour,
>   To travel across those gloomy straits
>   Those men from Labrador.
>   They had four dogs and a komatik
>   And a little canvas boat.
>   A mail bag and three nights' grub
>   And that was all she wrote."

He handed the fiddle back and started out again for Fifty-ninth Street. When they reached the park he turned and walked inside. A.D. angrily watched him go. "What kind of a joust is that? That might play in Hollywood or up there in Labrador, but that won't last an hour on my street."

Evelyn sat down on the same bench they had shared before, the one facing the Plaza. She shut her eyes, as if wanting to shut it all out.

"So I say, what am I fooling around making deals with him for?" A.D. went on, sitting down and impulsively picking up her hand.

"He might have one film left in him," she said, opening her eyes and looking at him.

He asked her if she wanted a drink and when she said yes he took her downtown.

"He must have put a special hook into you for you to put up with all his jive," A.D. said in the cab. "Great man that he is."

"No hook," she said and smiled. "When I was a kid we used to play a game called Green Gravel. We'd hold hands and go around in a circle. The person whose name you said would have to turn and go around with his back to the circle. Then we'd all sing:

> "Green gravel, green gravel.
> The grass is so green.
> And all the fair ladies
> Are shamed to be seen.
> Oh, *someone*, oh, *someone*.
> Your true love is dead.
> I'll send you a letter
> To turn 'round your head."

"Are you trying to tell me someone's dead?" A.D. asked as they got out of the cab at Sheridan Square and entered a dimly lit bar-restaurant.

"Not really," she said. "Just that I don't really believe in true love."

A thin, middle-aged black woman sat behind the piano and sang sad songs in a small plaintive voice. They sat through the set and had several drinks, and when A.D. asked Evelyn for her back story she sighed and said that she didn't like to get into any of that but then she had another drink and told him anyway.

"My father was Eskimo. My mother German. She came to Labrador as a nurse on the Moravian freight boat and she stayed on when she met my father. They started a trading post up on the northern end of Labrador, near Hebron. It was a lonely place, but there were five of us kids and we roamed pretty wild and never seemed to mind the isolation. When we got older we always made a point of coming home at the end of the summer and helping out however we could, and then we would all get into my father's boat and spend a few weeks hunting and fishing. This one summer I had come up from St. John's, where I had been laid off from clerking in a store and was waiting for an opening as a schoolteacher. Everyone was there but my oldest brother, who was off working on a trawler, so when we set off we had a full boat.

"Two days after we landed up at the inlet where we kept a fishing shack a big thunderstorm came down and the lightning struck the boat, went down the mast, burned a hole through the boat, and blew the radio to pieces. So we were cut off, but we didn't think much about it, my father going ahead fixing the boat while my two younger brothers went inland to fish on one of the lakes and maybe get some deer or caribou. I stayed around the shack with my sister and mother, helping my father a little and cooking and picking berries and putting in a supply of wood. It was all work we were used to and none of it was hard and we were having a good time when my youngest brother, Duncan, walked in and collapsed before we could get him inside the shack. He was shaking and having trouble breathing, and he said that my other brother, Early, had the same thing but was too sick to come in. A few hours later his lungs gave out and he couldn't catch his breath and he died. My mother thought it might be the Spanish flu, which is a terrible thing in those parts. One time it took nearly half of Labrador away in an epidemic.

"After we buried Duncan we set out for Early. We found him a day later and he was almost dead. My mother had her doctor's bag and she nursed him for two days, but finally he rolled over and died. By that time my mother had figured out it might be something to do with the water they were drinking, because the lake had a pink cast to it. People always used to say the army had dumped some chemicals up there years before and a few Eskimo and Indians had died from unknown causes, but no one ever did anything about it. My father told the Department of Lands and Forest but that was about it.

"After we buried Early we went on up to Joe Poquet's place, an old trapper who had a cabin by the head of the lake. When we found him he was lying on his bunk and he had been dead quite a while, because half his face was eaten away by weasels. Joe had written something on a piece of paper: *To the Finder. Everything I have is yours. Soon I'm a dead man.* We buried Joe as soon as we could, just wanting to get away from that place, and as we were about to pull out a seaplane banked in over the lake and came right out of the sun and landed in front of us.

"The first man out of the plane was Wesley. He was up there fishing with some of his Hollywood friends, and they were looking for Joe Poquet to be a guide for them, their other guide having been too much on the booze. They flew us back to the boat and spent a few days with us helping my father get the boat ready, and then they took off for Goose Bay and we sailed down there as well. I met Wesley in St. John's and one thing led to another and he offered me a job and, after holding out for two months, I took it and flew off to L.A., where I was his secretary before we got married. Although it wasn't really like that. There were a lot of in-between times, too."

"I'm sure there's a way to bank all of that," A.D. said.

Evelyn withdrew her hand from his. "I don't want to bank anything. I had been thinking of Joe Poquet and how he looked when he first walked in after a winter's trapping. He looked like Wesley did before he went into the park."

A.D. felt her slipping away and tried to pull her back. "Well, sure. Two brothers gone and then dealing with Wesley's losses. That's a burn, all right. Now, if it was me doing the song that's where I'd find my hook, in all that suffering. 'Oh baby, don't shut the door / On Labrador / Don't go away / with nowhere to stay'... But don't get me wrong. I'm not trying to cop your story. I have plenty of stories. I don't need yours. I love it. I'd use it. But I don't need it."

"That's good, because you can't have it."

A.D. held up his hands in surrender. "Hey. Believe me. I don't want it. No bad intentions. But just for Wesley, we should be traveling together."

"We can never travel together."

A.D. didn't break stride. "Of course not. We have different deals with Wesley. But we can acknowledge each other's position."

"Not even that," Evelyn said, standing up.

She looked down at him and started to say something, then suddenly turned and left. A.D. made no move to stop her. He'd go one more round with both of them, he thought, and if he came up empty he'd jump off the train and land somewhere else. That was one act he knew how to do.

OUT ON the road, Walker was having his own problems with images, unable to summon up a gesture, object, or even visual mood that might allow him to reenter the script. He had started to ponder the story, for one thing, questioning and trying to remember his own experience, and that had produced an almost instant paralysis as well as a smoldering rage toward his father for having trapped him inside such a hokey progression. Until now he had been mostly on automatic, letting A.D. prod him toward expressing some kind of form, however banal, that might lead him toward finding what he was looking for, not just if Clementine was alive or dead, but how he was doing as well. But as he traveled on, crossing the prairies and the Mississippi River and driving into the heart of Illinois and Indiana, his dread increased, finally causing him to veer off the road into a cornfield.

He stumbled out of the van, running between two rows of corn until he collapsed. Hugging the earth, he listened for the drone of an airplane. But there was nothing. Staring up at the empty sky, he shut his eyes. But no image appeared, inside or outside. He ran on until he collapsed again. He was halfway across the field before he remembered Cary Grant running through a cornfield in *North by Northwest*, a single-engine crop duster hunting him from the air. It was as if he had been unnaturally seized and he sat down and dissolved each image until the scene was erased from his mind. The effort exhausted him, and it was several hours before he backed the van onto the highway and drove toward the state line.

In Ohio he checked into a motel and had a long bath and half a bottle of Scotch before he let himself return to the scene in New Delhi with Lama Yeshe. They were images that carried a great deal more anxiety than Cary Grant running for his life through a cornfield, and he wrote them fast, without stopping, until he was too drunk to go on.

EXTERIOR. NEW DELHI — NIGHT... *Jim and Lacey drunkenly climb the outside stairs to the roof where Lama Yeshe leads a puja. Two dozen men, women, and children sit on thick narrow rugs decorated with snow lions and five-pronged dorjes or powerbolts. Lama Yeshe, or Rinpoche as he's commonly addressed, meaning "precious teacher," sits on a rug facing them, his body wrapped in a maroon robe. In front of him a small altar holds several rows of torma (sacrificial cakes), framed photographs of various lamas, and a clay statue of Padmasambhava, the Lotus-born guru. It is a relaxed scene, the children playing and crawling around, the women in their black chubas wearing jade and coral earrings and necklaces, the men in Chinese sneakers, cheap slacks, and short-sleeved shirts. Everyone praying with their malas or rosaries. Lama Yeshe looks up from the text he's reading aloud and strikes a hand-held drum as he nods to his assistant, a young monk with a shaved head who blasts out a triumphant note on a long Tibetan horn. Over all, a chaos of sound rising from the street, radios blaring popular Hindi songs from roofs and open windows.... To one side of Lama Yeshe sits the only other Westerner — Byron — clean and attentive in faded jeans and white shirt, his blond hair twisted together into a knot at the back of his head like Lama Yeshe's. Lama Yeshe whispers something to him and he makes his way toward the three strangers.... "Rinpoche will see you at the end of the puja," he whispers. Jim and Lacey wait until Lama Yeshe ends the ceremony, leading the invocations and prayers as they pass before him, palms pressed together, heads bent forward for a brief blessing. Afterwards, while they're drinking buttered tea and eating stale cakes and hard candy, Byron motions to Jim and Lacey to come forward. They sit before Lama Yeshe, whose small black eyes shift slowly from one to the other. Lama Yeshe asks where they are from, and when they say "America" he asks how big is it? Are people free there and if they are, how is that freedom measured? What is the color of freedom, the taste and substance of it?... Jim says he doesn't know about any of that, he's just Clementine's brother who has come over with his wife to find her.... "She is a serious student," Lama Yeshe says, looking at them while Byron translates.... Lama Yeshe and Byron talk back and forth until Byron explains: "Rinpoche says that Clementine's questions sometimes point to a beginner's understanding of the fundamental nature of mind."... "I'm glad if she's a fundamentalist," Jim says, "but I just want to find her, she hasn't been in touch with anyone in a year. Her father's worried. He thinks she might be dead."... Lacey interjects, "We're all frantic with concern."... "She's off on a retreat," Byron says.... "I don't care what she's doing," Jim says. "Purifying or polluting her mind or her body or whatever, I want to find her."... Again Byron and Lama Yeshe talk back and forth in Tibetan, with Lama Yeshe laughing and clapping his hands and offering Lacey hard candy from a plastic bowl. "Rinpoche says your view about purifying and polluting is quite correct and all experiences should be a source of insight. From that one taste you might begin to understand that form and emptiness are the same." Lama Yeshe then says something to Byron, who tells them to wait while he goes downstairs to get a letter from Clementine. While he's gone, they sit silently with Lama Yeshe.*

(Pop... I can hear you muttering, "Cut to the chase. That's where the money is." Which is true, I suppose, but in that moment something happened to Lacey. We were both drunk and disoriented and trying to stay on the point with Lama Yeshe when suddenly he leaned over to Lacey and snapped his fingers in front of her. She jumped as if she'd been hit but he just smiled at her, not taking his eyes from hers until she relaxed, which was amazing because I've seen her relax no more than five times in our marriage. About as much as I have with you or you with me. In retrospect I suspect that Lama Yeshe was trying to prepare Lacey in some subtle mysterious way for what happened later. Certainly in terms of the film I know you'd give such a prototype character as Lama Yeshe some flash, at the least a little prescience or holy mojo. So I'm not loading up the scene with messages and instructions about death. You'd automatically eliminate all of that anyway as, in fact, you do in your own life. But those demons were up there on the roof and Lacey must have picked them up because when Byron returned she started asking questions about death and what was going to happen with her after she died and how could she deal with her fear of death and so on. Lama Yeshe very sweetly gave her some textbook answers: "When death comes, if you have a relaxed mind you will be safe from the lower realms. Let go of whatever you might see or think and direct your attention upward, through the top of your head toward the light. Imagine the image of a precious deity above you and dissolve into the pure light of its essence."..."That's all very well for you to say," Lacey replied. "But I don't know how to do any of that. I don't even watch television."... Lama Yeshe very patiently explained it to her in another way: "When the moment comes, be like a child, not distracted or clinging to any thought, open but not active or emotional."... Finally Lacey's anxiety dissolved into a kind of temporary acceptance and Lama Yeshe asked Byron to read a section of Clementine's letter, which returns us to the script if we haven't been there already.)

...With Byron shuffling through the long letter he finally finds the one page Lama Yeshe wants to be read....."It's true, Rinpoche," the letter says. "My faith is so precarious that often I think I need a vulgar miracle to pull me through. My mind wanders and I have trouble with even the simplest part of the visualization you gave me. You warned me this would happen, that the purpose of this practice is the purification of obscurations, that original mind is encrusted with intellectual delusions and defiling passions and that the ego inevitably resists any attempts to purify it. Maybe so, but I'm still discouraged and resistant. My practice is willful and stale, and I have to force myself to do even a little bit. All I think about is packing my bags and getting on a plane for Bali or Goa and indulging every sort of hedonistic desire. I'm full of self-pity and narcissism, enough to wonder how a rich, fairly attractive young woman who just wanted to play the sitar in a rock-'n'-roll band and fall in love with the lead singer ended up doing prostrations alone in a cold damp shack in the foothills of the Himalayas. It's even worse than I'm saying, Rinpoche, because I'm too inhibited with you to describe my despair, which is not a good omen for our relationship insofar as it deals with surrender. But every time I think about surrender I always seem to end up shutting more doors. How can any of it work? We can't speak to each other without a translator.... Hi, Byron, Please write me. Your last letter made no sense at all.... You're caught in the stiff robes of formal religion while I'm caught in the naive mind of the deluded seeker. I keep wanting something from all of this, and the more I want the more I seem to fall apart. The most basic precepts elude me. I don't really know what is virtuous or what isn't, so how can I know what karma or cause and effect is? When I sit I don't really sit. When I listen I don't really listen. When I speak I don't really speak. I don't recognize my center of gravity, and my mind is endlessly full of speedy concepts that never give me a moment's peace. I have no idea what it means to attain realization, especially now that I see that those first experiences were nothing more than a slight crack in the outer layers of my conditioning. And yet I go on because I don't know how to go back. You say that the source of all phenomena is the mind, and true freedom comes from understanding that the individual

mind is fundamentally fallacious. But I have trouble in simply watching my mind much less understanding it.... So what am I doing about all these complaints? Nothing. I get up in the morning. I make tea. I do my practice. I take my medicine, although no one seems to know what's the matter with me. My prayers are empty and hollow. Who am I and why am I here is my only mantra. And so it goes...." Byron hands the page to Lama Yeshe, who replaces it in the rest of the letter. Then he reties the entire package with a red ribbon. Reaching down he touches Lacey lightly on the hair. He looks at her for a long time with such solemnity and compassion that it unnerves her until finally he stands and leaves the roof.... "Rinpoche showed you that letter as an example of what a serious student your sister is," Byron explains. "He also doesn't think you should meet her in Benares."..."Of course we're going to Benares," Jim says. "Especially now that she's sick and in some kind of depression."..."I wouldn't say it's exactly a depression," Byron objects. "More like a turbulent passage."...Jim is shocked by this casual attitude. "She's flipped out. All she talks about is what a miserable creature she is."...Byron spreads his arms, shrugging his shoulders. "Listen, I'm only a poor pilgrim myself, but I'm very close to your sister. Too close, actually. I would love to see her. I even need to see her, but Lama Yeshe knows her mind more than I or even you do and no doubt Clementine herself."...But Jim is determined. "At this point I'm not trying to find her mind, only her body. I just want to get her back home and then we can deal with all that other stuff."...Lacey places her hand inside his and they present a united front...."Well sure," Byron says sadly. "Good luck to you. By the way, do you need any religious artifacts? Offering bowls, tankas, statues, skull cups, butter lamps? Buddha's tooth? I'm raising money for a plane ticket to the States. One way, no return."...Lacey writes out a thousand-dollar check to Byron, who tells her Lama Yeshe might be going over as well. Impulsively she writes another check for a thousand and that closes the deal.... Byron takes the checks, writes his address on a slip of paper and hands it to her....

Evelyn sat in the dressing room of Conchita de Paragon, the ancient Peruvian actress, consort, and business magnate. They were both wrapped in terry cloth robes and sat together on a low divan waiting for their hair to dry. Beneath them, through latticed French windows, they could see Wesley sitting in a wicker armchair on the far side of the lawn reading Walker's last pages and occasionally firing a small hand-tooled Smith and Wesson at a target attached to the trunk of an oak tree three hundred feet away. A bemused gardener stood behind the bench, bringing back the target for Wesley's inspection after each round.

"You have read these pages?" Conchita asked. It was to her estate in Connecticut that they had come for the day, to return that night for a television interview that Wesley had agreed to.

"Last night," Evelyn said. "Wesley was too drunk to read them."

"His son writes the script?"

"Yes. There's another man that helps, a producer."

"What is the story?"

"It's about a man and his wife looking for the man's sister who has disappeared in India. So far they haven't found her."

"I don't think Wesley will make another film," Conchita said. "Not even with his family."

Very slowly she placed a cigarette into a long ivory holder, not bothering to light it. She was very old, and countless nips and tucks with the surgeon's knife around her eyes and in back of her head gave her face a haunted glacial look.

"He needs to work very badly," Evelyn said.

"Of course he does. That's why he's coming to me for money. He wants to hold on, to find some way to stop this terrible decay which is rushing on him like a black train. It's a great ignorance, this avoidance, unfortunately an ignorance which I share."

They had just emerged from the Jacuzzi, one of the many health aids and comforts that composed Conchita's vast and spectacular dressing room. Evelyn had never imagined a room like this one, with its sunken bath, sauna and steam rooms, stretch bar, high colonic table, racks and racks of clothes, soft Oriental rugs, erotic Picasso drawings, and inlaid Moroccan tiles. It was an inner sanctum, a domain that only a chosen few were ever allowed to enter, and Evelyn felt overwhelmed to have been ushered in directly out of the limousine while Wesley went off to the garden to read Walker's pages.

Conchita reached out to touch Evelyn's hair with a gnarled arthritic hand. "Your husband is a violent man. I used to know him well. We were lovers when he made that trashy comedy in Santiago. It was before his son was born, the son that now haunts him. The film was a disaster and he behaved very badly. No one would hire him afterwards. He would come to me and lay his head on my breast and suck at me like an infant. Very sweet and alarming. After that it was impossible between us as lovers, but on another level we have managed to be friends. He comes to me occasionally as he does now, to regain my respect because there are not too many people he can regain anything with any more."

"Will you give him your respect?"

"Of course. Every time. Even if it's not there. But not the money. I don't think he wants the money. He is a sick man. Not just the heart. Although I know he's had warnings. But his soul, that's in trouble. He does not have the energy or the will to see his way through such a commitment."

"Without a film to make he'll go up to Labrador and let himself die."

"Perhaps that is the best way. Men like him don't do well at the end of their lives. They are too attached to the world. When life finally fails them they become hysterical and a great stench rises off them, a great isolation. They are left with no image of themselves that is real, that they can depend on. They're like old mercenaries, unable to remember what side they fought on, who won the war, what it was even about. It has been my fate to love such men."

She paused to watch the gardener walk slowly to the target and remove it from the tree and walk just as slowly back to Wesley, who carefully looked it over.

"Why are you telling me this?" Evelyn asked.

"Wesley wouldn't have told me the truth, and I wanted to see for myself what kind of creature would be with him at the end."

"I've thought of leaving him."

"That would be foolish and sentimental."

"Maybe so. But I won't go back to Labrador."

"That is for you to decide. But I would try and remain somewhat in the boundaries of your marital contract. Wesley will leave you more than enough to last you for the rest of your days. He is chivalrous, in his way, and he has made a great deal of money over the years."

"Ever since I've come to this country all I've heard about is contracts. Making them, breaking them, looking for them."

"It's the land of the big deal," Conchita said without irony. "I embrace that cliché. It has gotten me this far in spectacular fashion."

"Then why won't you make a deal with Wesley?"

"Because that would be a very small deal that would never come to anything. I have complete confidence that Wesley will sabotage each effort to sustain himself as a man of action."

"You won't do any better," Evelyn said angrily. "You're certainly not prepared for the end."

Conchita looked at her gratefully. Rarely was she able to speak directly about the one subject that obsessed her beyond all others. "Ah, but I am prepared. I will do better even though I am older and have perhaps more fear and vanity than even Wesley Hardin. I'm like one of those fish that you find in European ponds that live for seven hundred years because they keep to the same slow steady rhythm and avoid all shocks. Which is why I must leave you now and why you must tell Wesley that I can see him no more. Somewhere in the next life we will meet again, but in the meantime he has my undying respect."

With that, she went out through a side door.

In the limousine going back to New York Evelyn told Wesley that Conchita had decided not to finance the film. He had not asked before, staring out the window and drinking bourbon on the rocks from the portable bar. He was wearing pale yellow slacks and brown Italian shoes and a soft and very old and frayed white shirt with a red bandanna around his neck. The way he sat, so contained within himself, caught at Evelyn's throat, and she thought she had never seen anyone so handsome and at the same time so lost and vulnerable. That made it all the sadder because at that moment she was beginning to feel that she might have enough courage truly to leave him.

"Why didn't she see me?" he asked.

"She couldn't handle the shock."

Wesley poured himself another shot of bourbon. "I thought she might have given something just out of perversity or amusement. It doesn't matter. I don't really care."

"What do you care about?" she asked. He didn't answer and she didn't ask again, knowing how those kinds of questions infuriated him. Instead she asked what he thought about Walker's last pages.

"I don't think anything about them," he said flatly.

"You must have thought something," she persisted.

His eyes narrowed, and she recoiled from his fear and anger.

"Everything, then," he said evenly. "I thought everything."

She forced herself to reach out and hold his hand. "Do you want me to leave, Wesley? I can, you know. I would be all right."

"Of course I don't want you to leave," he said quickly. But he wasn't able to meet her eyes, and she knew that part of him, at least, wanted her to leave and she laughed, thinking that perhaps in his mind he had already gotten rid of her.

"Evelyn," he said in a way that made her turn to face him again. "Don't keep asking me questions about living and dying and going to Labrador or not going to Labrador."

"I've never asked those questions."

"Maybe not, but they're always in the air. It's like asking me who I am. It's an insult. At this point I am who I am."

"You're impossible, Wesley. You don't play fair, and you never listen to anyone."

"I do with you."

"Not really. Only when you're bored or distracted."

"I'm not bored," he insisted.

"All right, you're not bored."

"Seriously, Evelyn, I'm going to do this script. It's all inside trains and rooms, and I'm a goddamn master at getting people in and out of trains and rooms. I can shoot it in Ceylon. I don't have to go to India. I can do the whole thing below the line for under six million. That includes freak-outs, travel expenses, doctor bills, and bribes. I have a meeting with an Indian businessman next week who has given me a verbal guarantee over the phone."

"I'm happy for you," she said as they both turned and looked out their separate windows.

The driver let them out in front of a run-down five-story loft building in lower Manhattan. Wesley, who had thought they were going to NBC, asked the driver if he had made a mistake.

"It's a cable station," the driver said. "It's where they told me to take you."

They walked up four flights to the top floor and were greeted by a thin young man in wire-rimmed glasses who carried a large manila envelope which he dropped as he shook Wesley's hand. Staring up from the floor were old publicity stills of Wesley kissing some of the stars he had directed.

"I'm hysterical," the young man said, bending down to pick up the stills. "I'm also your TV Host or interviewer or whatever."

They followed him into the studio, a small rectangular room with two swivel armchairs facing each other on a low stage against a background of false brick. In front of the stage two dozen film aficionados waited for Wesley's arrival. Among them A.D. and Sidney, with Sidney filming Wesley and Evelyn coming through the door.

Wesley put up his hands, experiencing real terror.

Sidney reacted by swinging around and shooting Evelyn and then panning the audience.

"Have you heard from your son and heir?" A.D. asked Wesley, holding a microphone in front of him.

"I read the latest pages."

"How do they play?"

Wesley didn't answer, watching Evelyn as she walked away to stand alone behind the audience.

But A.D. pressed on: "I can tell you one thing, the pages from Walker might be flat but your footage plays. When you're at your worst it plays better than when you're at your best, everything you do in front of the lens is magic, Wesley…"

Wesley didn't listen to the rest of it, walking over to the stage to sit down in front of the TV Host, who quickly introduced him:

"My next guest needs no introduction to a New York audience, having been much in the news lately with two separate lawsuits against M-G-M as well as several controversial public statements about the state of the film business in general and many of its more notorious participants in particular. He is also, of course, one of this country's finest and most successful directors, having made thirty-seven films. Among film buffs he's mentioned in the same breath with such legendary figures as John Ford, Howard Hawks, and Sam Peckinpah. He's also a man who has recently stated that the less said about the process of making films the better.... Wesley Hardin, I'm honored that you're here."

When Wesley didn't respond, the TV Host went on anyway.

"Given your aversion for interviews, do you find it a contradiction to find yourself here?"

"Where am I exactly?"

"Cable Television. *Notes Along the Celluloid Trail.*"

"I thought this was NBC."

"Would that make a difference?"

Wesley didn't hear the question, his attention drawn toward Sidney, who was standing at the back filming the interview. The idea of being manipulated inside someone else's film made Wesley suddenly thoughtful, as if for the first time he was actually considering the possibilities. The TV Host broke the silence with another question.

"When most of your contemporaries have either passed away or have retired, it seems remarkable that you should keep on making films."

"Not remarkable," Wesley said finally. "Sad, maybe, and boring."

"Even so, you must still manage to find satisfaction in the process. Otherwise why proceed, especially when faced with such obstacles as those you've suffered recently from M-G-M?"

"Bad habits. If I'm not on the trail of a story or a project, I'm anguished and full of rage. I'm convinced I'm going to die."

"In that case let's hope you're on the trail of a story."

"I am. It's at a very sloppy and intuitive stage, involving members of my family fooling around in a foreign locale. The producer is sitting right over there. He can tell it better than I can."

The Host feigned surprise and enthusiasm. "I see that he's also filming you. Is that part of the project?"

"I have no idea. You'd have to ask him."

"Speaking of your family, is it true that your daughter was named after John Ford's *My Darling Clementine*?"

"No. But I admire the pace and scale of that film. No one does work like that any more. He was secure in his beliefs, I suppose. You don't have a real drink, do you? Something that will get me through this?"

"I don't think we're allowed."

Wesley nodded as if he had heard something profound. He stood up, saying he would be back in a moment, but then changed his mind and called on A.D. to come up and talk about what they were working on. "I don't want to leave you in the lurch," he told the Host, introducing A.D. and then walking back to talk to Evelyn, who was putting on her coat. The camera stayed with A.D. and the Host, who was drawing laughs with his deadpan confusion.

"I take it you are the producer of this project?" the Host began.

A.D. was trying to relax and present a contained and authoritative image, but he wasn't succeeding. His eye kept darting over toward Wesley, who was standing against the far wall talking to Evelyn. At one point Sidney came in for a close-up and Wesley said something that made him turn and walk out of the studio.

"...and so, how did all this come about?" the Host was asking.

A.D. paused, as if gathering himself together, then smiled directly into the camera.

"I've always been a fan, you know? I've seen all the great films. And when I had a chance to put together a deal with Wesley Hardin, I jumped. Wesley wants to work with his family and I respect that. It's altogether a new process for both of us. A departure film. You won't have seen this kind of a story before from Wesley Hardin. I shouldn't say this with him over there, but it's so rare to work with a man his age who still hasn't lost it. I've learned a lot from him. I didn't know anything about film before I met him. I thought I did, but I didn't. To be able to put together a deal around him, well, it makes you think about yourself in a different way...."

A.D. looked over to see how Wesley was receiving all this. He was sitting alone in the back, Evelyn having disappeared.

"We don't mean to exclude you," the Host called out to Wesley. "Please, come on back, Wesley Hardin. We love you."

The crowd laughed and cheered, and when A.D. stood up to applaud Wesley as he stepped up onto the podium, they applauded as well.

ON LEAVING the studio, Evelyn hailed a cab and went directly back to the Sherry Netherland. After she had poured herself a drink she noticed Walker's manila envelope lying on the coffee table in the living room. The image of Walker out there on the road coming closer and closer made her finally open the envelope and read the enclosed pages, if only to learn when he might arrive.

EXTERIOR. NEW DELHI — DAWN...*Jim and Lacey are ready to roll, the Chrysler piled high with water containers, canned goods, camping equipment, suitcases, cameras, tape decks, and even a lightweight table and two folding director's chairs.... They drive through the parched desolate countryside, through town after town jammed with an endless* stream of people and the usual slow choked images of water buffaloes, cows, beggars, broken-down buses, etc. The tape deck plays Rod Stewart's "Standing in the Shadows of Love," and they sit back within the safe air-conditioned cocoon of the huge car, sightseers, voyeurs of a world they cannot touch, feel, or hear. . . . They slow to pass a funeral, the body carried on a freshly cut bamboo stretcher, wrapped in a grass mat and covered with flowers. Behind the body walk the mourners. For a brief moment they surge around the car, blinking at the strange apparitions inside. Lacey turns down Rod Stewart and they can hear the chanting: "Hare nam satya hai, Ram Nam satya hai." "God is truth." . . . But then the car passes through and the moment is just another image on the road. . . .

THE DAY IS A MONTAGE FULL OF SOFT DISSOLVES . . . the enormous blazing sun climbing to its zenith . . . the car penetrating farther into the interior, the tape deck blasting out The Talking Heads, Dylan, and the Clash, passing women and children swaying through undulating waves of heat, laundry and earthen pots balanced on their heads . . . . That evening they drive through another village of mud huts strangled in heat and poverty and disease. Beyond some paddy fields and mango trees they see flashes of color and activity. A festival is going on, and they drive over the narrow sandy road and park near an ancient stone reservoir, its crumbling tiers descending to a shallow pool of green slime. A large crowd from the neighboring villages wanders about the reservoir watching snake charmers, acrobats, puppet acts, and singers. The soft light has a melancholy effect and the festival seems part of a dream. Jim and Lacey are stared at as if they are visitors from outer space until finally they flee, pursued by a crowd of children. In the safety of the car they drive until they reach an empty field, the dying sun spread out on the horizon in a display of raw umber and vermilion too exaggerated to film.

EXTERIOR — NIGHT . . . They prepare dinner, cooling soup and beans on the propane stove and spreading out canned ham and bread on the flimsy card table they unfold from the trunk of the car. Jim opens up a jar of caviar and uncorks a bottle of warm champagne while Lacey lights a candle and places it in the middle of the table. They eat in silence. Halfway through the meal, more than a little drunk, Lacey asks: "Do you think

our marriage has a chance?"..."Not too much of a chance," he admits.
"We're not honest enough with each other, for one thing."..."You're not
going to play that old tune?" she asks angrily...."I don't want to. Believe
me." He boils water for coffee, tipping over a chair.... She won't let it
rest. "What do you mean, not honest enough? How can you say that after
all we've gone through on this trip?"... Something lets go inside him and
he says what he's thinking. "This trip is a Band-Aid. There are areas it
will never cover."... She opens up a bottle of bourbon. "Like what? Give
me an example."... He sits down and gives her an example. "Like sex.
We've become mechanical with each other."... She considers that. "What
else?"..."I can't stand your compulsions and the obscene amount of time
you spend indulging them. And sometimes I'm not too crazy about your
smell and the way you nip at me all the time and the silly little ways you
choose to distract yourself from taking anything too seriously."..."What
do you mean, my smell?"..."You get rank from time to time."..."Are you
finished?" she asks evenly...."No, but go ahead."..."For openers, you're
a creep for sabotaging this evening and starting something like this. I
was even having a good time and actually feeling positive about us.
But you always manage to pull the rug out from such moments because
you can't stand any kind of intimacy and will do anything to deflect it.
You complain that I'm distracted but you're paralyzed and the way you
embrace your paralysis is totally demoralizing."... Shocked by her own
intensity, she stops and they sit silently, gathering up energy for a final
assault. Night has fallen swiftly, almost brutally, and the candle on the
table flickers and hesitates. He stands and walks over to her, and for a
moment she thinks he's going to slug her. "Go ahead," she says defiantly
as he jerks her to her feet, bending her backwards and biting her neck.
As she struggles against him he kisses her. She gives in too easily and
this dampens him somewhat, but he gets beyond that and throws her to
the ground. She shrugs herself out of her pants and fumbles around in a
suitcase. "What are you doing?" he asks, taken back...."Looking for my
diaphragm."... Enraged he throws her down for real. "It's either right
now or I get in the car and leave you here," he explains, ripping away
the rest of her clothes...."Oh, God, fuck me," she moans.... In a fury he

mounts her from the rear and tries to do just that.... As they plunge on, the moon rises over them, the car and the paddy field visible as well as a crowd of spectators. Jim notices them first. "Darling," he says, imitating Cary Grant as he slowly withdraws. "Our enthusiasm seems to have drawn a crowd." Lacey looks up and screams.... She and Jim make a run for the car....

INTERIOR — NIGHT ... *Locking the doors, Jim throws the car into reverse, then jolts it forward, sending a shower of sand over the crowd. They find the main road and drive through the night. Lacey is hysterical, unable to stop sobbing. A shape looms before them and they swerve, missing a water buffalo. Jim slows, then speeds up again. Despite himself, he laughs, drowning out Lacey's sobs. "Well, I mean, after all," he says, and then they are both laughing uncontrollably....*

THE FOLLOWING DAY ... *finds them continuing on as before; the same dusty plains, mud villages, hollow-eyed children. They are sober and chastened, the Chrysler having become a mixed blessing, drawing attention everywhere even as it protects them. They pass through a small city where Jim wants to stay for the night, but Lacey implores him to keep going and so they roll on, the outskirts of the city looking as if a famine has recently swept through.... A few miles later a stone punctures the radiator and the car comes to a halt in a cloud of hissing steam. There is no sign of life except for a thin line of smoke in the distance. Lacey bursts into tears.... Jim shakes her. "This is no time to freak out. I'll walk toward the smoke until I find someone." Afraid to be alone, she decides to go with him and they lock the car and start off.*

EXTERIOR — DAY ... *The ground is full of short spiky cactus and piles of smooth boulders. Lacey, who is walking ahead, stumbles and falls.... As if in a dream, Jim watches a cobra sway up out of the dead grass, its tongue tasting the air as it slides toward Lacey, who is sitting with her legs crossed, holding her ankle. For a brief second she controls her breathing before her fear overwhelms her, her head beginning to shake. "Oh, God, please," she moans. As if in answer, the snake strikes, depositing its venom into her outstretched hand and in a long whipping motion disappearing into the dead grass.... Jim and Lacey sit watching each other. A hawk circles far above. A cricket chirps....."I'm dead," Lacey whispers. "How odd."...Jim kneels before her and tries to suck the poison out of her hand...."You have too many cavities," she says as she slips into shock.... He spits out what his mouth has collected. "I saw it in a movie. William Holden, I think. In Africa."..."Too late," she whispers. "Hold me. It's into my heart. The poison. Oh, please."...He breaks then, sobbing as he holds her in his arms.... She stiffens, eyes imploring him. But he can do nothing, only cradle her as the pain envelops her and the breathing becomes harsh and ragged and finally stops altogether.... He sits through the afternoon and evening, unmoving, unseeing, holding her rigid in his arms while behind him a collection of children break the car window and begin to strip the car of its possessions.*

Two YEARS later Walker sat underneath an elm tree at the end of a quiet residential street in Albany. He had been sitting for most of the day opposite Byron's apartment, the top half of a simple two-story blue and white clapboard house. He had gotten the address from the directory office at the local college where Byron taught an elementary course in linguistic theory. When Byron had not appeared by late afternoon, Walker finally rang the doorbell. No one was home. He walked around the house to the back, where a small dark-haired woman in a blue nylon jogging suit was pulling up carrots from a vegetable garden. He asked where he might find Byron.

"He won't be home for another few hours. I'm his wife."

Walker asked if she knew Lama Yeshe.

"Lama Yeshe?" The question had an unsettling effect. "What do you want with Lama Yeshe?"

"I knew him in India."

She stopped pulling up the carrots and walked over to him, wiping her hands on her pants. "You knew Byron in India?"

"I met him once. In New Delhi. How is he?"

"All right," she said in a way that implied the opposite.

"Look, you're not going to stay here, are you? The last person that came from India stayed for months and it wasn't good for any of us."

"I want to find out about my sister. That's all. Byron knew her over there."

She turned away, not wanting to meet his eyes. "Clementine?"

"Yes, I'm looking for her."

She wearily faced him. "Byron and I made a deal not to talk about anything involving India, Nepal, Sri Lanka, Thailand, or points east. I just haven't learned how to handle any of it."

"Any of what?"

She laughed, shrugging her shoulders. "Oh, you know. Karma and samsara. Lamas and their mamas. The Buddha, Dharma, and Sangha. The action of nonaction. Clementine. Enlightenment. Any of those hit tunes. But there I go, it's quicksand. Why don't you go and see Lama Yeshe? He'll drive you crazy trying to talk English and leave you more confused than ever."

"I only want to ask him one question."

"I know. He'll tell you, too. He works in a frame shop on the corner of Eldridge and Macy. You can't miss it."

Walker told her he would come back the next day to see Byron. Then he drove down to the corner of Eldridge and Macy. When he reached the shop the proprietress, an old woman with blue-tinted hair, told him Yeshe was in back. Walker found him stacking wooden crates against the wall. He wore blue jeans and a green golf jersey with a small alligator sewn over the breast. He had allowed a helmet of thick black hair to grow back over his scalp, although Walker noticed that the roots were white where an apparent dye job had worn off.

"Lama Yeshe?" Walker asked.

Lama Yeshe didn't answer, continuing to stack crates.

"Yeshe?"

"Ah."

"I'm Clementine's brother. I met you in New Delhi."

"Ah...Clementine."

Yeshe kept all stacking up the crates, refusing any help from Walker. After he finished, he separated a pile of frames into different sizes, hanging them on their designated pegs. Then he held up a frame for Walker's inspection. "My job," he said, his finger following the rectangular shape. Pulling a small dictionary from his pants pocket, he leafed through it until he found the word he wanted. "Image prison maker. No freedom for picture. Very good job. Freedom for me." He slipped into a red nylon warm-up jacket, and they went out to the front of the shop.

"Good night, Yeshe," the old woman said, looking up from where she had been balancing the books.

"Good night, Mrs. Orlovsky. You are happy?"

"Not happy, not sad," she said mechanically, as if they had gone through this many times before.

"Good," Yeshe replied.

"Not good. Not bad," she said.

"Ah, very best. You not fire me?"

"Not for all the black men in China."

"To the river?" Yeshe suggested.

They got into the van and Walker drove outside of town. The river valley was hot and they drove past apple orchards that were being harvested and dense fields of corn and alfalfa. After a while they crossed some railroad tracks and parked near a wooden pier. At the end of the pier a man and his small son fished for eels and beyond them in the river a speedboat went round and round in a large circle. It was only after they had sat down on a cement bench facing the river that Yeshe spoke.

"I remember Clementine."

"My wife and I were looking for her. My wife died and I came home. It's taken me all this time to find you."

"Your wife is dead?"

"Yes. On the road to Benares."

Yeshe looked directly at him and held up two fingers. "Wife and sister dead. Mother dead?"

"Yes. But you said Clementine was dead?"

Yeshe held up three fingers. "All women dead. Must take female inside."

"I beg your pardon?"

"Never mind."

"How did Clementine die?"

"Mind not so bad. Lungs very bad."

"Pneumonia?"

"Maybe. Anyway, dead."

The speedboat had stopped making circles and was floating idly in the middle of the river. "You said her mind was okay?" Walker asked. "Does that mean her death was free of pain and suffering?"

Yeshe walked over to the river's edge and poked around, returning with a cracked milk bottle. Placing the bottle on the bench next to Walker, he went off again, gathering up pebbles. When he had enough he came back and dropped them into the bottle. He shook the half-full bottle so that the pebbles made a loud rattle.

"Noisy mind," Yeshe said. "Much fear."

Then he filled the bottle up to the brim so that when he shook it there was no sound. "Full mind," he said. "No fear." Letting the pebbles spill out until the bottle was empty, he said: "Empty mind. No fear." Then he selected two pebbles and dropped them inside the bottle and shook it slowly so that there were only separate clinks. "Clementine's mind," he said and handed the bottle to Walker.

Walker filled the bottle halfway with pebbles and shook it loudly. "Walker's mind," he said. "Very noisy. Very scared."

Yeshe laughed and shook his head in agreement and they sat silently with the setting sun slanting in across the river. The speedboat had sped away somewhere and the man and his son who had been fishing for eels had left. No one was about except for an old woman in a faded yellow housecoat walking a puppy with a tightly held leash made from a piece of rope. The image of the old woman as she constantly yanked the puppy by the neck made Walker inexplicably sad and tears formed in his eyes. Yeshe wasn't watching, staring down at the ground and moving his lips in silent prayer.

"Never mind," Yeshe said. He took out a small notebook from his jacket pocket and tore out three empty pages. Handing the pages to Walker he asked him to "Write mother name. Sister name. Wife name."

Walker wrote the names and handed back the pages. Yeshe carefully folded them up, one inside the other, and put them in his pocket. Then he gathered up scraps of wood and newspaper and started a small fire. When the fire was going he handed the folded pieces of paper to Walker, nodding for him to throw the paper into the flames. After another round of prayers, he clapped his hands three times, and that was the end of it. Bowing to Walker, he walked away, down the railroad tracks toward the city.

"Wait," Walker cried, running after him. "I'll drive you home."

Yeshe whirled to face him, his eyes wrathful and unyielding. "Don't follow. You're the car. I'm foot."

"You'll get lost," Walker insisted.

"Lost?"

"Disappear. Separate. Become cut off."

Yeshe whipped out his dictionary and looked up the word. "No loose," he said and looked up another word. "No loose. No target."

"The city is your target."

"No city. Only one foot, then another. No one, no thing, no where. I loose all. Very good fortune for me. You stay and watch smoke. Sister, mother, and wife all go in smoke. Wave good-bye. Then walk loose forever."

With that he turned and walked down the tracks.

Walker watched the smoke until the fire had burned down to ashes. Then he got into the van and drove aimlessly through the countryside. When night fell he stopped at a roadside tavern and drank three rounds of straight bourbon. A *Star Wars* movie was playing at a drive-in down the road and he bought a bottle next door and drove in, turning off the sound and watching the images. The images didn't help, and he lay down on the seat and sipped the bourbon straight out of the bottle. When the film ended he stayed to watch the credits, looking for names that he knew. He thought he recognized the art director's name and possibly the assistant wardrobe man, but he wasn't sure. Everyone else was unknown to him. That was as it should be, he thought, and drove back to the motel, where he finished the bottle of bourbon.

The next afternoon he went to see Byron. He found him in the backyard near the vegetable garden shooting a basketball at a hoop with a wooden backboard and no net. He was wearing sneakers and cut-off jeans, and he wasn't as Walker remembered him. He had gained weight around the middle and his hair was cut short. Despite his labored breathing, he looked like he knew what he was doing on the court. Walker sat down and watched until finally Byron came over.

"Clementine's brother?" Byron asked. "I thought it was you. Although you seem changed. But aren't we all?" He held out his hand and Walker got up and shook it. "Did you see Yeshe down there at the shop or was he off somewhere watching the World Series?"

"I saw him."

"You're one of the few. He usually won't see anyone. I suppose he recognized you."

"I guess so, although I sure didn't recognize him."

"Well, no. He's trying out something new. Cutting loose from the old ways. At least on the surface. If I wasn't such an old, used-up disciple of his, he would have gotten rid of me long ago. He doesn't even let me translate for him. But forget all that. I'm sorry about your sister. What happened to you, that you didn't show up?"

"It's too long a story."

"Tell it anyway."

"My wife died on the road and I flipped out and ended up in

Benares stripped of everything and wandering around like some crazy American sadhu. Somehow I made it to Darjeeling and then up to Kathmandu, where I stayed in a Buddhist monastery outside of town. I just collapsed there, not doing anything but sleeping and eating. After six months I found my way home through Thailand and Hong Kong. I didn't learn about Clementine until yesterday from Lama Yeshe."

While Walker was talking Byron kept glancing at the upstairs window where his wife sat watching them. He waved tentatively but she didn't wave back.

"She's upset," Byron said. "We almost broke up last night on account of you, or rather Clementine. A few weeks ago she stumbled on some letters from Clementine when she was up in the Kulu valley. Your arrival opened up the whole thing again."

"But that's yesterday's news."

"They were amazing letters. They exposed a capacity for intimacy in me that my wife didn't know existed."

He picked up the basketball and threw up a long one-hander which missed the basket and the entire backboard. "Both Clementine and I were going through separate crises. She was scared and isolated and having experiences that she couldn't control or understand. I felt stuck and burned out with India and wanted to get back before I became too strange and out of touch. For a long time we were each other's only witnesses."

"Can't Yeshe set your wife straight?"

"She won't have anything to do with him. He doesn't care, of course. It's a mystery to me how I got involved with anyone who is so hostile to what I'm doing. But why go into that? I suppose you want to know how Clementine died?"

Walker nodded.

Byron put on a sweat shirt that was lying on the ground. "Let's get out of here. I can't stand to see her up there blasting me with her rage and suffering."

They walked around to the van, and Byron directed Walker to

a tavern ten blocks away. They ordered beers, and Byron told him about Clementine. It was the first time he had told any of it, and often he paused and stared down at the table or took a long sip of beer.

"Technically she died of pneumonia, but a lot of her systems had already given out and if it hadn't been her lungs it would have been something else. There had been signals about her health before, but she had always ignored them. We even fought about it, and I accused her of being impulsive about death. And it was true, she was fatalistic and passive and totally unprotective toward herself, which got her into trouble when she went off alone, which she often did. She took all kinds of chances, eating anything, trusting anyone, going anywhere. Yeshe was always scolding her about being undiscriminating and having the wrong view about service and sacrifice. She was doing a complicated practice offering up her body to all the sacred sources of refuge. Part of the visualization involves severing your skull from your body and then placing the remaining corpse inside a skull cauldron and offering it up. Clementine went for it like she was literally going to offer herself up. She was like a moray eel. Once she started chewing she wouldn't let go until she cut it right through to the bone. You almost had to sedate her to get her to stop. She had too much diligence, too much ambition, and she was as vain as a rock-'n'-roll star the way she set about trying to become enlightened. It was as if the more she believed all the brochures about Nirvana and all-encompassing wisdom-mind, the more knotted and twisted she became. I've been like that. One of those bushy-tailed pilgrims endlessly seeking until I got reduced by my own mind, which was inevitable, given my attachment to results. Since then I don't take anything for granted. It's just one step at a time now. One day at a time. This is a chair, this is a table, this is a hand, this is a story. It wasn't like that with your sister. Nothing was ever concrete. Nothing balanced. Everything offered up. A kind of reverse cannibalism. She had so much self-hate, but why get stopped there? What was so ferocious about her was the way she was trying to be holy. She was always worried that she wasn't authentic, that she was just another deluded seeker from the West strung out on spiritual materialism. Every morning before dawn she would go down to the river and buy all the fish that were half dead and set them loose in the river. She couldn't get enough of lepers and mutilated creatures, as if she were trying to take on the afflictions. On top of that, she was losing weight and beginning to look consumptive and her responses to people were too intense and compassionate, if you know what I mean? She was also having out-of-the-body experiences. Anything would set her off. A sound. Her meditation. The flight of a bird. Making love. We had to pull back on sex because she would often disappear into some other zone. She had to be grounded by a meal or her period or something on her mind. And even then she was a bliss junkie. Any sign of unity and she was gone. Once I thought she had crossed over altogether and I had to slap her and throw cold water on her. She thought of taking vows, of perhaps becoming a nun or going on a three-year retreat. More and more she felt the need to live inside a stricter set of prohibitions. But there were other problems, too."

Byron sat back and ordered another beer and then went to the men's room. On the way back he put a quarter into the pool table and shot down a rack of balls while Walker looked out the window at the parking lot. When Byron finally sat down he drank his beer straight down and ordered another one before he began again.

"So when Yeshe told Clementine to stop taking herself so seriously she took that as a rejection and took off for Sri Lanka. She was always taking off but she always came back. They had a lot of misunderstandings.... Look, the thing is, right about then they started to get involved. It was very intense. He was Lama Yeshe in those days as well as being married, and it upset a lot of people. Including me, of course. I was jealous and several times tried to leave, but Yeshe refused. He simply kept me there. And he made us all look at each other without mercy. To leave I would have had to give him up as my teacher. Because there were a lot of other things going on as well. Yeshe's relationship to his wife, Clementine's spiritual crises, my own breakdown. Not to mention Clementine's being so disturbed about your father. His rejection drove her into a very extreme place and she was consumed with guilt as well as real bone-shaking relief for finally getting rid of him. I don't want to run him down in some kind of ignorant way, but he did cut her loose like he was limbing a dead branch. To top it all off, she managed to get pregnant. She didn't know whose child it was, mine or Lama Yeshe's. There was no question about having it, given the precepts that we were all committed to, and Yeshe decided that she should go off to the mountains with me and we would all three take responsibility for the child and that we would think about it in a positive way. Clementine and I got into a terrible fight. I couldn't stand Yeshe's posture of holy omniscience and the way he kept shoving his equanimity in my face, although in retrospect I can see that he was having his own problems with his wife, not to mention the Tibetan community, which was properly scandalized. But I felt betrayed and hurt, and my whole relationship with him as my teacher was in question. I couldn't see what benefit this soap opera had for any of us. And Clementine had given herself up to a holy mother role and that annoyed and isolated me even more. When I told her she was just another example of shallow mysticism, she went off and left again, going up to the Kulu valley for a three-month retreat.

"Two months later she had a miscarriage. She was very sick, and the local doctor thought she was going to die. She refused to give him anyone's address, but he found a letter from me and wrote me in Delhi. Yeshe wanted to go, but for various reasons it was impossible, and I went alone. When I got up to the little village she was living in, she wasn't there. She had left no forwarding address and not even the doctor knew where she had gone, saying only that she had been totally distraught and he was worried about her mind. When I got back to Delhi there was a note from her saying that she was in Benares and that she wasn't well but she would survive and that Yeshe and I shouldn't worry. But we were worried, and a few days later when you showed up Yeshe had very strong premonitions that your wife was headed for some kind of disaster and that Clementine had either died or was going to die. So the day after you left I flew to Benares.

"It took a week to find her. She was in Sarnath, an hour outside of Benares. She had gone there on a pilgrimage and was living in a government bungalow near the Deer Park, where Buddha preached his first sermon after attaining enlightenment. She was in one of those small rooms with a string bed, a bare light bulb on the ceiling, and no plumbing. It was clean enough, but it was next to a bus station and there was always a lot of noise. She was lying on the bed when I came in and didn't know who I was. She had lost about thirty pounds and had chopped off her hair. I sat down on the bed and held her while she went limp in my arms. Finally she recognized me and was able to say my name and whisper that she was glad I had come. You apparently had never made it. I figured that you had seen how hard it would be on the road and had turned back. And then, to tell you the truth, I just forgot about you. It was clear that Clementine was dying. I tried to get her to a hospital or at least to a good hotel in Benares where I could get a doctor, but she refused. I thought of forcing her, but then I gave in because I was afraid that she would just die en route if she didn't want to go. I fixed up the room as best I could and put in a mattress so that I could sleep beside her. She refused to eat anything but broth and some soft-boiled eggs that I made on a little kerosene heater. She had a few dharma books and I read her passages from the Bardo Thodol and recited prayers and mantras, particularly 'Om gate gate parasamgate bodhi svaha'—Gone, gone, gone beyond, completely gone. I had never witnessed anyone's death and even though that's what the trip is supposed to be about, I felt unprepared. Clem was lying there on the bed way out beyond language, staring at me with her huge eyes as she slipped in and out of her body. I bathed her and tried to match my breathing with hers and after a while there was nothing else. I whispered what I could remember of the Bardo instructions, but I couldn't tell if she heard me or not. At the end of two days and nights she opened her eyes and looked at me, forming 'Yeshe' with her lips, and then she turned her head to the wall and died. I had prayers said for her and saw that she was burned properly. I wrote you about her death, care of that address you gave me in Beverly Hills, but obviously it never got to you. And after that I forgot while Yeshe and I set out on our own pilgrimage through Australia, Hong Kong, Chicago, and finally here."

That was all Byron cared to say. They sat around for a while and shot a game of pool, and then Walker took Byron home.

The next morning Walker drove to Vermont, intending to make a swing through New Hampshire and then down through Massachusetts and Connecticut before arriving in New York.

WHILE Walker was on his leisurely detour, Wesley and Evelyn were hanging out at the end of the Seventy-ninth Street Boat Basin in New York, contemplating the sleek and elegant yacht *Eastern Star*. It was a cool Sunday morning and the hint of fall was in the air. They were wearing matching outfits of blue Topsiders, wool-knit turtlenecks, and waterproof canvas pants, and they were both hung over and hesitant about being on the water, even on a structure as obviously well appointed and seaworthy as the *Eastern Star*. They had just about decided to pass and go back to bed when A.D. appeared on deck. He was dressed like a Marlboro ad and he was smoking a huge cigar.

"Ahoy there," A.D. yelled down at them.

"I'm not going on board if there's a camera around," Evelyn said very quickly to Wesley.

"We've been getting great stuff," A.D. went on as if he hadn't heard Evelyn. "A give-and-take interview with our host, Toulouse, who is my kind of high roller, and now we're going to establish the two of you coming on board."

"The camera in its case and the key in my pocket," demanded Wesley. "Or we're gone."

Sidney appeared next to A.D., wearing his safari jacket and cradling a 16mm camera in his arms.

"Wesley, consider the location," Sidney said patiently. "We have a classic visual with you against the skyline saying what New York means to you, what films you've made here, what triumphs and disasters you've experienced. That kind of thing. Then we segue inside the boat with you firming the deal with Toulouse or maybe sabotaging the whole thing or who knows what?"

Evelyn reacted to all this by walking down the dock. Immediately Sidney locked the camera in its metal case and threw the key to Wesley. After Wesley had handed the key to Evelyn and she had thrown it in the river, they went on board, following A.D. and Sidney down a mahogany ladder into a spacious, softly lit salon.

The furniture was an odd combination of South Indian, contemporary Swedish, and Ethiopian. Formica tables and foot stools made from zebra and rhinoceros hides stood before low couches covered with silk patterns from the Bhagavad Gita. On the walls Indians and cowboys galloped through nineteenth-century paintings of frontier life in the Far West.

A large man with shiny black hair and a thin mustache rose to meet them. He wore designer jeans and a pink cowboy shirt with pearl buttons, and he looked not so much Indian as Eurasian.

"Fabulous," he said, shaking Wesley's hand. "It is a great honor. I know all your films frame by frame."

"How unsettling, " Wesley said.

"Not at all. A great satisfaction. But I'm sounding like Sydney Greenstreet. Please, sit down, Mr. Hardin, and your charming wife. Yes? Evelyn, I believe."

They all sat on a couch and Toulouse pushed a button in an intercom and told the captain to cast off. At the same time a steward presented them with champagne and plates of caviar and smoked salmon, serving as well a party of five Asiatic men and women who occupied a corner on the far side of the room.

"One of my teams," explained Toulouse. "For reasons of health and temperament, I have been at sea for the past several years and I arrange for my advisers and experts to fly in and visit me at regular intervals. That way I don't become stale. Perhaps you do the same with your team? I have spent a good deal of time with them these past few days, and I must say I have found them to be candid and illuminating.

"But now I want to speak to you directly about the script, if that is possible? Good. I assume I may call you Wesley in the casual manner of the film community? Wonderful. First, Wesley, let me say again, from the bottom of my heart and soul, that I adore your films. I have an entire collection in my personal archives, as well as a record of everything you've said or written in public. So you see I am an aficionado. I love your passion and your fearless appreciation of the banal and ordinary, even your occasional violence, and I would be fascinated to see what your particular vision would do with a subject as vast and different as India. Such a film would be an important cultural and historical bridge. But on reading the script as it now stands, several reservations come to mind. Even though I am obviously an amateur, I can foresee how difficult and taxing such a film would be to make, and I'm not sure that it would be wise to undertake such an expedition, especially given the present state of your health, which your staff has kindly filled me in on. But more to the point, perhaps, is the script itself. Frankly, I find the two central characters dull and uninspiring, and I am unable to relate at all to the girl they are looking for. Clementine, I believe her name is. Also sex and religion are rather complicated subjects in India, and the script is highly offensive in both areas. There would most certainly have to be radical revisions to gain official approval.

Your team has suggested adding another girl, to create a sort of theatrical triangle as a way of reducing the emphasis on a spiritual search, and also introducing some much-needed humor. I approve wholeheartedly."

"I'm always open to discussing change," Wesley said.

"Your team has assured me of that, and I find it immensely gratifying to find someone that I am in such awe of to be so available and communicative. We would, of course, bring in another writer. I have in mind a chap from Bombay. Very fine on local dialects and Indian customs. Very amusing fellow. Understands the subtleties of East and West. Also in terms of my money situation, having him would be most agreeable. My next point is really my main point. I am committed to pursuing the Indian project without a doubt, that is, of course, if everything can be worked out to our mutual satisfaction. But I am absolutely excited and overwhelmed by your current film, the one you are now shooting. Your team has shown me excerpts and I think it is very fine, very precious stuff."

"What film?" Wesley asked.

"The one that you're now shooting. This one. Here and now. You and your wife and son and the final breakup with the studio. Wonderful, wonderful footage. Shocking, really, the way you allow your whole life to be on the line, or not to be on the line. We shall find out which. But it's wildly amusing as well. We must not abandon that project."

"I haven't seen it."

"With that in mind, we have prepared a little *soupçon* for you of various moments in various places."

Toulouse pushed a button that turned off the lights and another one that started a projector, a screen unrolling from the ceiling as they watched....

...a close-up of Wesley standing outside the saloon in Durango, a small spill of light from the window highlighting his chest but leaving

his face in shadows. Members of the crew pass, some shaking his hand, others ignoring him.... The Prop Man, dangerously stoned and looking for trouble, embraces Wesley with both arms. "Say the word, boss, and I'll sabotage the trucks and get the studio man busted at the border."..."None of them matter that much," Wesley says. "I was losing it anyway. Could you tell?"..."Well sure. I could tell for some time. This isn't an old man's game. Will the girl stay?"..."Evelyn? For a while. Until I fuck up."..."Which you will," the Prop Man says. "But there are others to take up the slack. What about that old broad in Mexico City?"..."No more replays," Wesley says.... The Prop Man embraces him again and moves on.... Finally Evelyn appears. "Where the hell have you been?" Wesley asks angrily. "I've had to stand here like I'm saying good-bye at my own funeral."..."I lost my purse."..."Oh, Christ, that's all we need."..."Are you the only one that's allowed to lose anything?"..."At this moment, yes."... The camera focuses on him as he walks alone down the empty street, past the jail and the bank and the telegraph office.... Evelyn and Wesley sit at the airport bar, surrounded by the Production Manager, Assistant Director, Leading Man, and Art Director. "What will you do after Mazatlán?" the Production Manager asks Wesley.... "I don't know. Write my memoirs. Look for my daughter. God knows where she is but she couldn't be any more lost than me."..."Hell, you're not lost, Wes," the Leading Man says, desperately hung over and confused. "You went down with your guns blazing."... They drink silently, not knowing what to say. From behind the camera Sidney asks: "Where do you think your daughter is?" ..."My daughter? I don't know. My son says India, but my son has been known to say one thing and mean another. Maybe we'll both go over there and take a look. She's a strange girl. Independent and willful. Like me, I guess. I don't know about either of my kids, to tell the truth. I suppose they'll come back to haunt me now."...Wesley walks on the beach at Mazatlán, holding a black umbrella to protect him from the sun.... Sitting in a bar, he looks straight into the camera: "I'm not going to sum up my goddamn life. Absolutely not. And fuck you for asking me."...On the beach at night, Evelyn and the Frenchman from Mexico City sit around a fire. They have been swimming and are wrapped in large beach towels…"Do I love Wesley?" Evelyn asks. "You can't just stick the camera in my face and ask questions like that."…"Why not?" Sidney asks.…"It is an invasion," says the Frenchman. "How would you like it if I asked you questions?"…"I wouldn't mind."…The camera changes hands.…"What you do is obscene and childish," the Frenchman says. "How can you defend yourself?…"

Unable to watch any more, Evelyn rose from the couch and walked out of the salon, Wesley following her.

They stood on the stern deck, the yacht moving slowly down the river toward Battery Park and the open harbor.

Wesley was the first to speak. "If everything I do causes you such pain perhaps we should think about separating."

"Is that what you want?"

"It's not what I necessarily want but it seems to be what's happening."

A.D. came on deck and stood off by himself, smoking a cigarette and staring down at the ship's wake.

Wesley spoke again: "Does your silence mean you have decided not to communicate on any level?"

"I'm considering that possibility."

"It was a mistake for you to come. These meetings never mean anything."

"It has been a mistake from the beginning," she said sadly.

"I'm not altogether sure, but I don't think so," he said.

Stooping down, she took off her sneakers and handed them to him. It was only when she was almost over the railing that he figured out what she was doing.

In a long dive she cleared the yacht and started swimming for the shore a few hundred yards away.

"Someone stop her," A.D. yelled.

"It's okay," Wesley said calmly. "She swims like a seal."

A.D. was furious. "If we had a camera we could get that shot. It's a one-in-a-million shot."

"It's a meaningless shot if you don't know what you're doing, and if you had a camera she wouldn't have come."

"You blew it with Toulouse," A.D. said. "It was a bad time to split because the next scene was his favorite. You remember the party at the Frenchman's house in Mazatlán? You listed your favorite films and were vicious about other directors, putting down the whole business. Then that South American critic busted you for not having any dignity."

A sailor had run down from the bridge and was yelling for the captain but Evelyn had already reached the dock and was climbing up an outside ladder.

Wesley called out to the sailor: "It's a bet we have on. Don't worry about it. It was prearranged."

The sailor went below to report to Toulouse.

"Some woman you have there," A.D. said. "A real animal. Does this mean it's quits between you two?"

"I don't know. Maybe."

"I'll tell you one thing, she's a bummer for the project. I've never heard that woman put in a good word for you."

"I suppose not."

"As one of your partners and all-time fans, I sure hope you can hang in there. With Toulouse, I mean.... He'll pick up the tab and give us a location trip to India. That way we can shoot you finding Clementine and reuniting with Walker as well. You know how much this means to Walker. That boy has worked his guts out being on the trail of this story. Right now he's probably up there in Albany with one of those religious fanatics. There's nothing he's not going to do to make a connection with you. I don't see how we can let him down. I believe in this project, Wesley. This is it for me. I waited my whole life to find this one."

"I'm not interested."

"Maybe that's true," A.D. said quickly. "Maybe you're not interested. But that doesn't mean you can't still keep it alive. Blow a little smoke up Toulouse's ass. Sidney and I have put a lot of time on this project. We haven't been drawing wages either. We're going for broke. And you might not know it, but life on the street isn't too colorful these days."

Wesley felt a quick slice of pain in his shoulder and a shortening of his breath and he leaned against a bulkhead and waited until the sensation passed. "I'm not feeling all that well," he said. "I'm going to lie down in a cabin somewhere. You do whatever you have to with Toulouse. I don't care. Just don't tell me about it."

"That's good enough for me," A.D. said.

He helped Wesley go below and find an empty cabin. Then he went back to Toulouse and tried to make a deal.

As soon as they docked, Toulouse's chauffeur drove Wesley back to his hotel. Evelyn had not arrived yet and he sat for a while on the living room couch with the lights off. He was still numb and disoriented, but much of the dread had slacked off and suddenly he just wanted to get out. He wanted to leave this darkened room and then the hotel and then no doubt the city and after that it wouldn't matter. He went into the bedroom and packed a bag. He had three thousand dollars in cash and he left five hundred for Evelyn and wrote her a check for five thousand more. "Going North" he wrote on a room service menu and left it on the bed. Then he took the elevator to the street and walked aimlessly down Fifth Avenue. After forty blocks he took a cab to the airport, but it wasn't until he told the driver to stop at Air Canada that he fully realized he was leaving the country. The first flight available was to Montreal and when he arrived it was ten at night.

He booked a room at the Holiday Inn and slept all that night and the next day and night, and when he awoke the following morning he knew what he was going to do. In a department store he bought a large duffel bag and filled it full of long underwear, wool shirts and pants, and other durable clothes suitable for the far north. Then he took a cab to the airport, booking a flight to Stephenville, New-foundland, where he hired a float plane. The float plane took off straight into a vicious sunset, and thirty minutes later Wesley rec-ognized the blunt shape of Slab Island squatting in the Gulf of St. Lawrence like a massive battleship. There was still enough light to distinguish a small pod of finback whales making their way north toward the Strait of Belle Isle. When he was a child the Inuit had killed them just for muktuk, the slabs of skin and blubber they loved to chew on, and it moved him now to see the whales pass-ing the island. The plane flew over French Tickle, the long narrow fiord cutting into the heart of the island. Beneath him were forests of fir and black spruce and the same barrens where he had slogged through miles of bogs and lichen heaths hunting for caribou and moose. He thought about the island and how little it had changed. Fewer changes than he had gone through in his life. No doubt. First there had been the Portuguese whalers who had been forced to winter there. After them had come the trappers and shipwrecked sailors, and then the Inuit and Beotucks, attracted by all the action, had drifted in to trade. The only change after that was a hundred years later when the Brethren of the Moravian Church, unable to resist one of the bleakest places on earth, firmly planted their mes-sage on the simplicity and total practicality of God and never left.

It was the white frame structure of the Moravian Church that Wesley looked for as they banked and flew in directly over the long wooded bay. When it wasn't there he panicked and thought of his namesake, the eighteenth-century convert John Wesley, who had witnessed the profound calm of the Moravians on a voyage from

England to the New World. Faced with a violent storm off the coast of Labrador, the ecstatic pilgrims had sung hymns in terrifying transports of joy as the sea poured over the gunwales and the mainsail split in two.

Wesley took a pull from his half-empty bottle of rum and quoted John Wesley's observation of the Moravians to the pilot: "I can conceive of no difference between a smooth and a rough sea, except that which is between a mind calmed by the love of God and one torn by the storms of earthly passions."

The pilot nodded pleasantly at the old drunk as the pontoons settled gently over the water and they sped across the bay toward Tilt Cove, a settlement sheltered from the north wind by somber granite cliffs.

There was only one boat out, a small open dory, and the young boy standing at the tiller waved to them as they passed.

"Going home?" the pilot asked.

"Going home," Wesley said.

"You'd have to pay me to live in a place like this." The pilot feathered his engine and brought the plane around so that it glided up against the wooden dock.

The usual crowd of kids and old-timers were waiting for the plane. One of the old-timers recognized Wesley.

"It's Wes Hardin."

"Well it is."

"Been on the outside a good long time."

"In the States, from what I heard."

"He'll be going to the house."

"I guess. Where else would he go?"

One of them called out to him and Wesley was afraid to look, nodding and tossing the bottle over as he climbed out of the plane. A sharp wind came in gusts from the northwest, and his entire body felt the chill as he walked down the dock, behind him a gang of kids fighting for the privilege of carrying his bag.

All was not as he remembered. The first change was the gutted cannery at the end of the dock and past that the Moravian Church, which looked like a movie set, nothing remaining but the front wall, a TV satellite disk standing among the rubble where the building used to be. A thick silence hung over the town which made him oddly apprehensive until he realized there were no dogs, that snowmobiles had done away with the need for them. Before there had always been a constant howling and barking, but now there was only the odd sound: a shout, a burst from a chain saw, the slam of a front door. There were prefab houses now and the Hudson Bay Post was new, a large Quonset where the old barnlike structure had stood, but everything else seemed the same. The town was still divided between whites on the west end and Inuit and Indians on the east end. There were still no streets, the houses scrambled about in gullies and declivities among the pitted black boulders and rocks. Salmon and char hung from clotheslines and a variety of new and busted snowmobiles, boat engines, and water pumps lay scattered everywhere.

He walked through the town, past the Hudson Bay Post and the old shingled houses that had held the same family name for over a hundred years. Stopping to rest after every few steps, he climbed the steep hill in back of the town until he stood winded and dizzy before an ancient two-story house whose paint had long since peeled off and whose peaked gabled roof was exposed to patches of black roofing paper. Two of the upper windows were covered with plywood and a two-by-four had been nailed across the front door, but a thin line of smoke rose out of the chimney and a light was on in the kitchen. He gave the kid carrying his bag a dollar and went inside the kitchen door.

The kitchen smelled of spoiled fish and the floor was caked with dirt. Kindling had been dumped in a loose pile near the door and plastic was nailed over two of the rear windows where the panes had been broken. Wesley recognized the Enterprise woodstove and the black kettle on the back burner, but there was a man sitting in a chair near the icebox that he had never seen before. He was very old, with a curtain of thin white hair framing his face. Half his teeth were missing and a long scar slanted one eye, pulling down the corner of his mouth. His heavy cord pants were held up by rope suspenders and the top of his long johns was stained with grease.

He looked at Wesley with pale rheumy eyes. "If you be government, you can leave right now. I got no regrets. The man cheated me on my pelts. I'll bust him in the windpipe again if'n I feel like it."

"I'm Wesley Hardin."

"You ain't."

"I am."

"I'll be the last man in hell. Come in and set."

Wesley put down his bag and sat on a chair. Accepting a bottle of rum, he took a long pull and handed it back.

The old man drank and shook his head, his eyes never leaving Wesley. "Meat's meat but you don't look like no Hardin."

"I suppose not," Wesley admitted.

"You ain't knowin' me?"

Wesley shook his head.

"Long Hatcher, that's who." He looked at Wesley with his mouth open, a hollow whistling sound pumping through his toothless gums.

"Long Hatcher?"

"The same. You ain't looking good, Wesley. Not worth the price of powder, my son."

"I'm tired," Wesley admitted. "Figured I needed a change."

"Don't we all, my son, don't we all. But the Slab be the wrong place for change. Everything be going the other way. Cannery shut down. Ten cords of pulp won't buy a pair of boots and a bottle of rum. Salmon fished out. Government telling us we can't hunt the seals. Oh, it be hard times, all right."

"Will you put out your traps?"

"Not this winter. Don't make a whole lot of sense, price of pelts being what they are. No, Wes, I'm telling it straight. Feels like lately I don't own nothing but my own breath, and that's going fast."

"How long have you been in the house?"

"Since your mama and daddy died. A good thing, too, or they would have stripped her down past the nails. Word has it you've been down to the States."

"Mostly."

"People say there's work there. You must have done all right to have stayed this long."

"I made enough to last me to the end."

"A man can't ask for more'n that."

"I don't suppose."

Long's breathing had become labored and he was unable to speak, shaking his head and spitting up gobs of phlegm on the floor. Wesley sat with him, smelling the room and starting to open up to it and then pulling back. He took an ax leaning against the table and split up a pile of wood into kindling. When he had finished with the wood Long's breathing had evened out.

"I'll sleep upstairs," Wesley said. "You don't have to bother with me."

"And don't you bother none about me," Long wheezed. "I'm squeezed in at the end of the pantry. Got me a mattress and it's right handy."

Wesley went up the wide stairs, which were worn in the middle, and turned into a large room with a peaked ceiling and a dormer window that faced the sea. The only light came from an uncovered bulb on the ceiling. Dust covered everything, and there was the smell of urine and a stronger, bitter smell as if a small animal had died. Black glass from Captain Morgan rum bottles drifted up against one wall and the window had been nailed over with punctured plasterboard. A brown army blanket full of mouse holes lay twisted on the bed. He recognized the chest of drawers and the large oak desk that had been taken from a French schooner wrecked off Tilt Cove a hundred years ago, but initials other than his had been carved into the headboard of the bed. Turning off the light, he lay down and pulled the blanket over him. Where were his children this night? he wondered. He had trouble breathing and he turned on the light and went over to the window, punching a hole through the plasterboard with his elbow, enough to allow a cold rush of air into the room. On the way back to the bed he cut his foot on an angle of broken glass. Making a crude bandage with his shirt, he huddled beneath the blanket, trying to remember how it had been getting up before dawn and going down to the kitchen, where he and his father would eat silently and then walk to the dock. Other men would be there and they would take the boats far out into the night so that when dawn came they would be out of land's sight. Sometimes they would stay out through that day and the next night before they would come in. But now it was another night in another time, and he was forever separate from all that but no more separate than from the day that had just ended. Toward dawn, he fell asleep and when he woke a few hours later he felt calm enough to make his way to the kitchen.

Long Hatcher was still sitting by the stove.

"I've been waiting for you for some time," Long said. "Since your mama died anyways. I wanted to sing my song for you before I went under myself. I heard your mama's and daddy's song and now you'll hear mine. It's only right."

Wesley agreed and they drank tea in silence and then Wesley went upstairs and fell asleep. He slept until midday and when he came down to the kitchen again Long was lying drunk on his mattress. He tried to prop himself up on his elbow, looking at Wesley with rheumy imploring eyes as if he had something of great importance to say, but then he fell back and passed out. Wesley was grateful to sit in the kitchen unobstructed, to let the feel and memory of the room settle over him. But there was still a gnawing restlessness inside him, still this forlorn sense of futility and despair, as if the actual sameness of the room, the same chairs and cupboards and the same oak-planked table and yellow bone-handled knives and forks, conspired to make him feel even more separate, as if coming back had been nothing more than cheap sentiment, another ludicrous dodge against confronting whatever inner layers of himself still remained. He drank another cup of tea, adding a large dollop of rum, and then it was no longer possible to remain inside. Changing into long underwear and woolen pants, he put on his new fur-lined boots and Hudson Bay parka and, taking a shotgun down from a rack over the door, he stepped outside.

Climbing up the hill in back of the house, he made his way inland, skirting a long U-shaped bog and heading for a dense thicket of elderberry bushes. The day was windy, full of bleak rain-filled clouds scudding off toward the northwest. Years before, at this same time of year, he had followed in his father's footsteps as they went hunting to lay in meat for the winter. They would go out every day for weeks until the weather turned too raw and bitter, and even then they would sometimes continue if the game had been scarce. Those were the only times he had felt a bond with his father, although they rarely talked and then only at night, after they had skinned a rabbit or partridge and sat eating around the warmth of a fire. Sometimes his father would permit him inside the rigid boundaries of his fierce containment. Talking slowly of the past and his father and his father's father and how they had always hunted this land and how as long as there were Hardins the land would belong to them. What great failing had caused Wesley never to allow his own son to follow, however briefly, in these same footsteps? Or strength, he thought savagely. Because it was over, all of this, it was only sport now and an old man's ambiguous anchor to a past that Walker could and should have no use for.

A rabbit scampered in front of him and he raised his shotgun only to lose his aim as the rabbit darted off to the side. As if to test his resolve, he fired a round at the sky, the report shocking him and for a brief moment emptying his mind. He walked on, through the elderberry bushes and into the dense spruce forest that stretched for sixty miles to the other side of the island. It was quiet now inside the refuge of stunted windswept trees, and he sat down against a lightning-split trunk. He dozed and when he woke there was a light rain falling and there, through the trees, stood a slender doe, her head and flank exposed.

As he raised the shotgun, she turned toward him, her eyes and nostrils shuddering with fear. And then he fired, the pellets striking her head and neck. But she wasn't fully dead, and plunging through the woods, she disappeared from his line of vision. He followed her to the edge of a steep ravine. He could see the trail of blood and hear her shuddering death agony beneath him, but the ravine was too steep for him to descend and once down he knew he would never be able to get back.

He sat on the edge of the ravine until he couldn't hear her any more and then as the day turned suddenly, almost brutally dark, he made his way back, his body shivering under stinging gusts of rain.

Long wasn't there when he got back, and he built up the fire in the stove and dried himself off, hanging his clothes on the drying rack overhead. Then he went up the stairs once more and lay in the dark listening to the rain until sleep finally rescued him.

In the morning when he came down again Long Hatcher was sitting by the stove.

"Is there still a boat?" Wesley asked. "I'd like to go out in a boat for a short while."

Long walked over to the highboy and took out a full bottle of rum. "For the boat. The best of the rest."

Wesley made a pot of coffee and fried up some potatoes while Long returned to his chair and fell asleep, snoring loudly. After Wesley had eaten, he stepped outside and walked around the house. The house had been built and added to over the years with lumber taken from wrecked ships, and its joists and beams were all solid oak. Although Long hadn't bothered to bank it, the foundation seemed firm enough. Wesley sat down on the front steps and watched narrow avenues of fog drift in from the sea. Once in a while the sun broke through, lighting up the frost-shattered rocks.

Long came out. He had put on wool pants and a yellow mackintosh and was holding the bottle of rum. Wesley went back into the house and returned with his down jacket and a black toque that he put on his head, and then he and Long walked down the steep hill into the town. A few figures nodded and called out but he didn't recognize them. Fish had been washed and lay stacked on wooden racks waiting for the sun to dry them. Long stopped to take some squid out of a barrel for bait, wrapping it in newspaper. Then they walked halfway down the dock to the *Angie D.*, a wide-beamed dory with an open cabin. An old woman wrapped in a black coat sat against the Chevy motor in the middle of the boat, drinking coffee from a thermos.

"Get out of my fuckin' boat," Long stammered.

"I have a right to see Wesley Hardin," she said calmly. "More than you, that's for sure."

They stepped down into the boat and Long primed the motor. The old woman ignored him, taking off her wire-rimmed spectacles and looking up at Wesley with a toothless grin.

"You don't remember Annie Mae?" she asked.

Wesley didn't remember.

"You and me and Long been down the river a time or two," Annie Mae said knowingly. "We were in goddamn grade five together. Then there was that time we were swapping spit up at Huckle's Point and old man Poultry come by, him that got caught on the ice in Thunder Bay."

Wesley cast off and Long guided the boat slowly into the harbor. A loon flew over, disappearing into a pocket of fog, and then puffins and a razor-billed auk passed by. The boat cleared the harbor and they went past a line of breakers into the open sea. There was a gentle swell on, and they sat quietly as Long cut the engine and dropped anchor.

"You must be bringing TV to the Slab," Annie Mae said as they set their hand lines with squid, jigging them fifteen fathoms down.

"Not me," Wesley said.

Annie Mae chose not to believe him. "Heard you was bringing in twenty-eight stations. All from the States. I think you came back to the Slab to do just that and it's a great thing and it's what I come to tell you. I'm an old girl and when I can't get about no more TV is goin' to be my company. I ain't goin' to turn it off until they find me stiff as a salted cod."

Annie Mae poured coffee from her thermos into tin cups and Long added large dollops of rum and they drank and waited for the fish. A migration of murres, looking like diminutive penguins, cackled maniacally as they flew past.

"You surely must be some wizard of wrong notions to come back to the Slab," Annie Mae said. "Nothing here to do but die."

"Nothing wrong with that," Long said.

"You're goddamn right." Annie Mae shook her fist at both of them. "Take Wesley Hardin's own grandpa. I was a little bitty thing, but I was there. Times was hard. Nothing to eat. Takin' bets on who would make it through that winter. Now old Grand-daddy Hardin knew he wasn't worth a lick in hell. Never helped out. Never had nothin' good to say about nobody. Was ugly to boot. Finally he seen the light. Got properly likkered up and commenced to go to each and every family. He had his tell on those he knew and they on him and everyone had to have their share of eating and drinking and passing out so it took more than three days and nights for everyone to wind up at the Hardin house. I know you recollect the night, Wesley, because you was right there when your own pa took a sealskin rope from a chest and threw it over that stringer you got running across the living room. Most all the town was looking when Granddaddy Hardin stood on a little table and put the noose around his own neck and said he'd done the best he could, take it or leave it, and that he looked forward to never seeing their goddamn faces again. Then his own son kicked the table out from underneath him and he swung free, dead as a stone."

"That's the way it was," Long affirmed. "An April night and warm, too."

"Course the TV will change all that," Annie Mae said. "Different kind of entertainment going on now. Not many around knowing how to go out the old way."

Just then the fish started to hit and they spent the next few hours laying in a quintal of cod. After they had rolled up their lines, Annie Mae split up two big tom cod, taking the airsacks and backbones out with swift cuts and throwing them overboard. She made a little fire over some rocks in the bottom of the boat and put the fish in a pot with fatback pork and onions and potatoes and cooked them in their own juice. When they had finished eating and were working on the last of the rum, a plane flew over, sliding down through the fog for a landing.

"Not a month goes by when you don't see one," Long complained.

Long lay down and fell asleep while Wesley and Annie Mae sat staring off across the sea, with their backs on opposite ends of the Chevy engine. It was very still and they were content just to sit there. Their peace was broken by a cool breeze that stirred up the swell and caused Long to wake up and start the engine.

Three hundred yards from the dock the fog lifted, and they could see the plane and a large crowd on the dock.

"God's grace," yelled Annie Mae. "It's the TV folk come to plug us in."

But it wasn't the TV folk. It was A.D. and Sidney and another man working the sound. They were wearing new camping outfits and they had the camera on a tripod, pointing it toward the *Angie D.* like a weapon.

"I don't want nothing to do with it," Long said.

He sat down and it was left for Wesley to steer them in. He didn't succeed, the bow slicing into the dock with a loud ripping sound and the boat immediately filling with water. The end of the dock collapsed and two people slid into the freezing water. Everyone else stood at the safe end of the dock applauding and calling out advice.

The camera crew continued shooting as Annie Mae and Long

were helped out of the boat. Wesley got out on his own, crawling up on the dock on all fours.

"An historic approach," Sidney said, zooming in on Wesley.

"We made the deal of a lifetime with Toulouse," A.D. explained to Wesley. "He's passed on the Indian project, but he's picking up the entire tab on your footage. He thinks it'll be a great film."

"He's not picking up my tab," Wesley said.

"Your tab, everyone's tab. It's carte blanche."

"It's my film and it's not carte blanche."

"We can iron all this out later," Sidney said. He put down his camera and began to change film. "We've been getting the crowd ready for you. Most people don't know what the hell you've been up to all these years. But now that we told them you were bringing in the TV satellite they're crazy about you. You're the lord of TV, the holy messenger bringing the outside inside. We've laid out three cases of booze for a party tonight in your honor."

Before Wesley could object, a florid-faced man in a Sears, Roebuck hunting jacket shouldered his way through the crowd and shook his hand. "I'm Pagels, the Hudson Bay man. One of your producers just now filled me in on the film you're doing and how it ties in with the TV and all the benefits that will be coming our way. Wesley Hardin, I just want to say for all of us that you being back on the Slab is the best thing that ever happened, and we're putting on a big Welcome Home to prove it."

Long poked Wesley in the stomach. "I seen all this coming years ago. I been second-sighted all this time, but you're the one that's lit the fuse."

He took Wesley by the arm and guided him through town to the Hudson Bay Post. Rum and Scotch and beer were lined up on the counter and there was already a large crowd inside, with the rest of Tilt Cove coming in behind them.

"I been down this road, too," Long muttered.

He took a bottle of rum and went over with Wesley to sit by Annie Mae, who was propped up on a pile of feed sacks on the other side of the cavernous room. The movie people were interviewing old-timers on what they remembered of Wesley and picking up background shots. Wesley watched them maneuver toward him, the camera panning over to include him.

"How do you feel about being home after all these years?" A.D. asked, shoving a microphone in front of him.

Long answered for him. "He don't feel a goddamn thing. Can't you people see he's already got one foot in the misty beyond?"

"In that case," A.D. asked Wesley matter-of-factly, "what are your last words?"

Wesley turned away, experiencing underneath one of his many blankets of humiliation a ludicrous little tug of joy. Meanwhile the rest of the party was gaining momentum. An old Indian was tackled from behind as he tried to stagger outside with a hundred-pound bag of flour. Inuit and Indian children threw food at each other while Pagels and his wife tried to secure as many canned goods as they could before they disappeared off the shelves. The crowd applauded each antic, word having gotten around that the tab was on Wesley and the TV people. Someone turned a radio all the way up, John and Yoko singing "Every Man Has a Woman Who Loves Him," and no one paid much attention when a large fat woman fell through a window.

Suddenly, unexpectedly, Wesley passed out. A few hours later he awoke to find only half as many people present, but they were there for the duration. The kids had gone and it was quieter, with more steady drinking going on. A few people had already passed out on the floor and a fight had broken up a display counter, but the Hudson Bay man and his wife had managed to protect most of their goods, sitting up on the counter near the cash register with shotguns cradled in their arms. The camera crew was shooting from the floor at an old man climbing up on a stove by way of a wheelbarrow and a water pump. He wore greasy bib overalls, rubber boots, and a snap-brim leather cap. His long block of a face was bitter and sad and no one listened except the sound man as he stared out across the room and spoke his piece:

"I'll say this about Wesley Hardin. I knowed him them days, never since, but I was one of the first to see him go astray. We was twenty years old and working as oil rats down in the whale factory at Poke Harbour. We was boiling out the oil from whale in twelve-hour shifts and making good money, too. We worked all that summer and into the fall and then we went over to Newfoundland, figuring to trap all winter and come back on the spring thaw. It was the first time either one of us had been that far away and we was raw about it but we knew what we was doing. We portaged in a hundred miles, carrying two canoes and four months of food. Built a first little tilt for me and then Wesley went on forty miles with the idea we'd meet up after a few months. As soon as I had put out my traps I noticed Wesley took damn near all the sugar with him. You understand what I'm saying? Anyways, I lit out after him. Damn right. Walked three days to get to his place. When I come into his tilt mad as a teased snake, he was laying on his bunk and you could see right away he wasn't right. He didn't even look at me. He just lay there staring at the ceiling. The whole place was a mess. Mice and coons were all over the place. He had him a nice little stove of galvanized metal and there was a terrible backdraft and he hadn't bothered to fix it. It's a wonder he didn't freeze. I fixed the place up for him and all the time he didn't say a damn word. Not that I wanted him to. When I finished I asked him was he going to set his traps. He says: 'Lemuel, I'm going to go as far from here as possible.' And I says: 'Wesley, you're already as far away as possible.' Then I walked out, but not before I took all the sugar and a few other doodads as well. I figured he wouldn't be needing them. I took the man at his word. He said he was going on and I let him go. As for me, I took most of his clothes, rifles, ax, and a sack full of food. That was the last I heard or seen of Wesley Hardin until he showed up just now looking the same as when I seen him last. So I say: Howdy, Wesley. How you be, old son?"

Lemuel waved to Wesley and fell off the stove, twisting his leg but not enough to keep him from limping over to the counter for a drink.

A shrunken white-haired woman in an old army coat stood up on the counter near the cash register, clearing her voice and speaking out in a loud voice: "Now I knowed Wesley Hardin and the others, too. Coley Hardin and Dan Louis Hardin most of all. I recollect the winter of 'thirty-two. The Spanish flu was on and it was down to lean pickings or none. We was living with the Hardins that winter in the Macy house. All three of us families was there and it was some hard...."

Her voice faded and the party seemed to lose momentum only to pick up again with the arrival of three young trappers all loudly drunk and shouting for the secession of Labrador from Canada and the entire Commonwealth.

Wesley stood up looking for a way out but was intercepted by Sidney and A.D. Once again A.D. presented a microphone to Wesley and once again it was rejected.

"A message from Walker taped last night," A.D. said, his voice strangely hollow and subdued.

Wesley received the statement as if it were a physical blow and sagged against a sack of feed. A.D. hesitated and turned off the tape recorder, but Sidney stopped him, turning it on again and then moving in with the camera for a close-up on Wesley's reaction.

"...It's two-thirty a.m. and I'm sitting in the Sherry Netherland with Evelyn and your home movie crew. I'll take part of the responsibility for A.D., but Sidney is your contribution to the culture. I'm wired and stoned and distraught to know that, once again, you've disappeared. But I'm not going to Slab Island. That's for sure. I can't speak for Evelyn. She's taking a bath. I'm sliding along a raw edge right now and it makes me want to give you more information than you asked for. Such as: I spent the night in Montauk with Evelyn. It was very sweet and we both needed each other and I, for one, don't have any regrets. I'm sure she won't reveal any of this, as protecting you seems to be an obsession with her. But you're bound to get the news when they screen all their demented

footage for you. Although that night might never happen the way these guys are shooting. They remind me of that lame comedy team you used for the killers in Baby Legs. *Totally inept and perverse. If I were you I'd take all the footage away from these goons as soon as possible. They seem to think that violation means reality, but then who are we to say no to that? In fact we've said yes all along. But why am I saying all this? Why is it still so important for me to communicate with you when you have never met me halfway, never once? And why do I bother to tell you that I made love with your wife and that it's okay and we're not going to run off with each other? Perhaps because it was your choice not to be here when I arrived, not to receive the final information about Clementine, and to leave me staring into a camera, which, I admit, I consented to do. So I say: You want to know what I'm up to? How I can serve you in terms of a story? What my back story is and how you can transfer your children into one-dimensional images? Fine. Here it is. And here's the story about Clementine. Then our deal will be over and I'd appreciate a check as soon as possible care of the Sherry Netherland, which is where I'll be until I figure out my next move, which I suspect might be back to Albany en route to who knows and who cares where.... Wait. Here's Evelyn. She's out of the bath and wants to say something...."*

"Wesley? I trust you'll be somewhere, sometime at the other end of this machine. But I suppose Mr. A.D. Ballou will see to that. He looks determined enough. I don't feel right communicating this way, but it's the way it happened so it's the way we have to go. There are things Walker didn't mention, doesn't know how to say, but that he said to me. Perhaps because saying it is some kind of release—for me, for him, for both of us—from you. Do you know what I mean? Saying that we love and hate and fear you? Giving each other permission to say those things and feeling that all of us, including you, have come to the end of something? So you're leaving us together makes it possible for all of us to go our separate ways. You know that I can't follow you to Slab Island. I can't go back to that even if I owe it to you. But you know that it wouldn't be good with us and anyway, that's not why you're there, is it? You can always come back if you want to see me. I'll be here or somewhere where you'll be able

to find me. But you won't come. I know that, too. No regrets, Wesley. Nowhere do I have any regrets, and I pray that your own regrets are fading, have faded...."

Wesley stood up and walked to the back door and stepped outside. There were northern lights and the sky was full of red and silver flares. Still drunk, he walked aimlessly through the town and out to the end of the dock. After a while he stepped down into the *Angie D.*, sitting on the Chevy engine and looking out over the harbor, the black water oily and unsettling. He felt himself to be waiting for something, a terminal sign perhaps, some small acceptance of that lost silence within that was now threatening to rise and wash over him completely. But there was nothing but the idle chatter of his mind: vague images and fragments of dialogue that could just as easily have been from one of his films as from his actual life. He sat until the cold had numbed the push of dead language and empty scenes. Then he walked slowly back to the house on the hill.

They were waiting for him: Annie Mae and Long and the usual cluster behind the camera and a dozen others that had struggled up from the Hudson Bay Post. They had brought the radio and they were all drunk, except for Sidney, who kept his cold eye behind the lens, focusing on Wesley as he walked through the kitchen and collapsed on the torn and split living room sofa.

A.D. sat off to one side, holding a bottle of rum in both hands and staring vacantly out the window. Sidney, who had apparently taken over and whose eyes shone with a malicious and heightened resolve, approached Wesley with the camera, the sound man carrying the tape recorder.

"Do you want to hear the rest about Clementine?" he asked. Without waiting for an answer, he gestured for the sound man to turn on the tape.

Where were we? On the road to Benares with Jim. Dazed. In shock as Jim sits by the side of the road, his arms wrapped around him, shaking and afraid. The next morning he has gathered himself together enough to stumble on. He walks all that day down the blistered empty road not knowing where he is, where he's going, where he's been. Outside a small town he buys tea and a stale chipati with one of his few remaining coins. Unable to eat, he retches violently and staggers into the middle of a field. Somewhere within the extremes of a paroxysm that involves his whole body he experiences a release, a chaotic letting go, and he lies thrashing on the ground until the seizure leaves him empty and oddly still.... Surrendered for the moment to whatever awaits him, he joins workers from a cement factory piling into the back of a flatbed truck, their exhausted bodies covered with white dust.... Hours later the truck stops and they all disembark, Jim following an old woman as she pushes her way into an ancient bus. He manages to say "Benares" to the driver, who nods and points up the road, accepting Jim's gold watch as fare.... A day later, the bus rolls into Benares. Dazed and on the far side of exhaustion, Jim attaches himself to a small band of naked sadhus walking to the Ganges for their evening prayers. Suddenly they are pushed and pummeled by a deluge of worshipers as saints, cripples, lordly palanquins, dying pilgrims, magicians, and religious hustlers, all the variations and then some, accompanied by booming and clashing cymbals, stream through an ancient gate and throw themselves at the holy river. Jim feels caught within an awesome hallucination, abandoned to a force that is incomprehensible and cruel. As he sags against a crumbling wall, he stumbles over two corpses lying on a rope charpoy wrapped in white and covered with flowers. A sheet has fallen away revealing a child's face painted red. He has stumbled into the land of the dead. The air is thick with smoke from a wooden pyre where a body lies burning, a gnarled gnomelike creature popping open the skull with a long stick. The air has the sweet and pungent smell of a pork barbecue and Jim feels faint and nauseated. He sits down near another body, which lies waiting on a wooden rack, dressed in white robes, the shriveled extended face neither man nor woman. Two men casually pick up the rack and place it on the pyre and the ghat at-

tendant touches the wood and there's a crackle of flames as the fire licks upward. It soon reaches the body and the belly opens and the intestines ooze out. The feet burn to a black crisp. An arm falls off and the attendant takes his long pole and expertly flips the corpse over.... Jim flees to the edge of the sacred river. Hymns to the dead echo from a half-sunken temple above him. Worshipers wade in front of the ghats chanting, "Rama, Rama, Hari Rama," sprinkling water over their heads, caressing with little intimate mudras the flat surface of the river. The whole shore is packed with walls, ancient turrets and balconies, stone platforms and apartment houses.... Jim wades in up to his shoulders. Squatting down, he lets the thick oily water cover his head. A dead cow floats by and on the far shore beyond a progression of enormous low-flying cranes he can see smoke from other burning ghats. He dunks himself over and over, obsessed with the sensation of being completely covered. After one particularly violent dunk a hand reaches out and grabs him by the collar and he's dragged roughly to the side of a houseboat, one of many stretching along the shore connected to each other by ropes and wooden planks...."Your ablutions were getting a little excessive," says a voice with a soft German accent. "I hope you don't mind. None of my business of course."...The voice belongs to an emaciated man with a long blond beard wearing only a rumali, or G-string. With great effort he manages to pull Jim into the boat.... Jim lies panting on the warped planks while his savior regards him from underneath a torn green canopy. Finally the strange figure speaks: "Perhaps you might care to join me for tea? I assume you are English or at least English-speaking?"...Jim nods weakly and the German helps him climb down a ladder into a rectangular low-ceilinged room. It has a spare, simple arrangement: a few straw mats, a kerosene stove and a bucket of water, piles of cloth-bound books and candles placed about on the floor. Jim shrugs out of his wet clothes and is handed a worn and faded dhoti. As soon as he's seated he sags against a wall unable to keep awake. "Rest," his host says. "There is no need to speak."...Jim sleeps while the German lays out his clothes, efficiently going through his pockets. Miraculously Jim has retained his billfold. There is no money, but there is an identification card and a snapshot of Clementine, a thin blond girl in a tennis outfit. There is also a copy of Charles's report and a card with a list of telephone numbers on it, including Jim's father's.... Several days pass in a series of dissolves showing... the German performing a series of vigorous asanas... bathing in the river... smoking opium while studying a book of sutras... spooning Jim clear broth, carefully cooling his forehead with a damp cloth... taking a ricksha to an international hotel where he places a call to Jim's father.... The dissolve ends with Jim revived enough to sit on the deck of the houseboat and eat a few spoonfuls of rice from a wooden bowl. The German waits until he has finished before he tells him what has been going on: "You have been out of your mind for several days. During that time I have taken several liberties. Through a friend I have located your sister in Saranath. My friend says your sister is very sick, maybe dying. If you feel up to it, we should go there immediately. I have also called your father and he will arrive this evening."... "Why are you doing all this?" Jim asks weakly.... "Your father is rich," the German replies. "We have made a suitable arrangement for my services."... They take a taxi to Saranath, the German dressed for the occasion in clean white slacks and a white shirt. He points out the great Stupa where Shakyamuni preached the first sermon after attaining enlightenment, quoting the opening lines of the Dhamapada: "We are what we think, having become what we thought. Like the wheel that follows after the cart-pulling ox, sorrow follows an evil thought."... "Are you hustling me?" Jim asks.... "I don't think so," the German says. "But then I am an ignorant man and my intentions are often obscure."... They find Clementine at the end of a narrow street in a tiny two-room flat. Before they enter her room, the German talks in Hindi to an old woman preparing soup in the kitchen. "She thinks your sister will die tonight," the German says.... Clementine lies on a cot in a clean whitewashed room. As they approach her, the German steps back, letting Walker sit on the chair by her bed.... She is extraordinarily thin, her skin bleached and nearly diaphanous, her hair cropped close to her skull. Her thin parched lips are slightly open, her eyes closed, as if she has already gathered herself for the journey within.... "I leave now," the German says to Jim. "I will meet your father at the airport and bring him here."...As soon as he's *alone Jim lies down on the cement floor and falls asleep. When he wakes, Clementine is staring down at him from the bed, her dark eyes huge, translucent. He sits on the chair and holds her hand.... "Oh, Jimmy," she whispers in a voice so low he has to bend to hear her. "Is Lacey here?"... "No," he says. "But Pop is coming in a few hours."... The news unsettles her enough so that she tries to sit up, but the effort exhausts her and she sinks back again, shutting her eyes. Jim feels a compulsion to do something, going into the kitchen and bringing back the soup the old woman has prepared. But Clementine is unable to accept even a sip and he puts the bowl beside the bed. Not able to sit quietly, he walks over to her small altar on the other side of the room. The offering bowls are full, and a butter lamp casts a soft glow over a photograph of Lama Yeshe and a reproduction of the peaceful deity, Dorje Sempa. A pile of dharma books is stacked off to one side and Jim brings two of them back to the bed, thinking that he might read to her, but she shakes her head. "No time," she manages to say. "Just sit with me."... He sits with her and for a moment isn't sure if it isn't Lacey lying there until Clementine's lips slowly form the words: "Pray for me."... He nods and waits a long time before she is able to whisper again: "Keep the lamp going. Forty-nine days... sweet brother... No words. No thoughts.... Light."... She sinks back inside herself and he waits, not daring to move until she moves, which she finally does, groaning softly through a perilous exhale.... She sleeps and he sits with her until the German arrives with his father.... Old Pete has lost weight and his eyes and mouth are lined with fatigue. But despite his obvious exhaustion, he presents a brave front in his blue and white seersucker suit and bow tie.... He sees that Clementine is asleep and turns to end a conversation with the German. "I absolutely refuse to give you cash. A check will have to do."..."It is not me that cannot accept a check," the German says, holding his ground. "It is the Indian bureaucracy."... Finally Pete gives him ten one-hundred-dollar bills and the German leaves without a glance toward Jim or Clementine.... "Now then," father says to son. "The first thing we have to do is get her out of here and into a hospital. Failing that, to a hotel suite where we can bring the best doctors."... "Too late," Jim says.... "What do you mean, too late?"..."I mean too late. She can't be moved."... For the first time since he stepped into the room Pete looks directly at his son, shocked by what he sees. Jim wears the same faded dhoti that the German gave him and an equally faded blue kurta that hangs loosely over his waist. But it is Jim's sunken ravaged face that upsets Pete the most. He cannot bear to see such exposed and vulnerable grief. It embarrasses as well as frightens him. Shaken, he sits on the chair by the bed looking down at the shrunken form of his daughter. "Where's Lacey?" he asks numbly.... "Dead," Jim replies, his voice empty of any emotion. "We were driving here from Delhi and she died on the road."... It is too much for Pete to handle and he slumps in his chair only to rally a few minutes later. "All right," he says stiffly. "It is tragic but we must go on. We must get a doctor here immediately."... "No." Clementine's whisper resounds through the room and they both turn toward her. "I'm dying, Pop."...."I absolutely refuse to accept that," Pete says, fired up now that he has something to fight for. "You must not give in."...A smile passes briefly across Clementine's lips and she makes one last effort. "But I must. As you must...Even you, Pop."... She lies back then and as Jim and Pete kneel by her bed, her eyes are already beyond.... Jim turns to his father. "She's dead."...*

At this point the sound man turned off Walker's tape, not because it was finished but because Sidney was no longer filming Wesley's reaction, having swung the camera up toward Long, who was standing on an end table with a noose around his neck, the rope having been thrown over a wide oak rafter.

"I don't see the use in haranguing.... I seen enough and heard enough. But I'll tell you one thing, Wesley Hardin. Your blood is mighty thinned out. My son ain't no different. Bought him a saloon in Labrador City and the truth is, he ain't cut out for it. Now me, I'm dead meat. Deer is deer and moose is moose and I'll soon be belly up."

He paused to take a slug from a bottle of rum and Sidney chose that moment to take the microphone from the sound man and push it toward Wesley.

"Do you have anything to say about any of this?" he asked Wesley.

A.D. provided the answer as he lurched across the room and picked up an ax leaning against the wall. With one blow he smashed the sound equipment and then went after the camera.

At that moment Annie Mae chose to pull the table out from underneath Long.

All movement in the room stopped as Long swung free. For a suspended moment he hung in the void between life and death and then the rope came loose from the rafter and he dropped to the floor.

Sidney made a move for the ax and A.D. reacted by swinging the ax down and chopping off Sidney's right index finger.

Sidney's howl filled the entire room.

The Hudson Bay man, well versed in such matters, wrapped Sidney's hand in a towel to stop the bleeding and forced him to drink a full glass of rum.

"You cost me my trigger finger," Sidney screamed at A.D. "You've ruined me and you've ruined the film."

A.D. looked at him blankly, not fully comprehending what he had done.

"I'll sue your ass," Sidney said weakly as he was led away by the Hudson Bay man, followed in turn by the sound man and the rest of the subdued revelers.

Long picked up Sidney's finger and put it in his pocket.

"You never know when a man might need an extra dick," he said as he shuffled slowly into the kitchen.

"Does all this mean TV ain't coming to the Slab?" Annie Mae asked.

"Sooner or later it will come," Wesley said. "You can count on it."

"I'll be first on line," Annie Mae said and followed Long into the kitchen.

Wesley sat down on the sofa and regarded A.D., who stood alone in the middle of the room still holding the ax in one hand.

"Tomorrow I want you and the rest of your crew off the island," Wesley said wearily.

"I'll be the first to leave." A.D. dropped the ax at his feet and stared through the window at a thin slice of moon that hung up in the sky like a whore's earring. "But I didn't know Walker was going to pooch your old lady. I never listened that much to what he was saying."

"It doesn't matter," Wesley said.

The answer seemed to confuse A.D. "I guess it doesn't. I mean, everyone takes on everyone in the end, don't they?"

"No, they don't," Wesley said. "But maybe they should."

"I'll destroy the rest of the film," A.D. said. "I can do that. The only thing is, I don't want to go back to what used to be."

"No need for that," Wesley said absently. "You take the film and do what you want with it. You're the producer and I trust you implicitly. Better an old demon than a new god, as they say. But there's no need to deal with India, production costs being what they are over there."

A.D. nodded and walked across the room to sit on the floor opposite Wesley, his back to the wall. He shut his one eye and then opened it again. They sat there in silent communion, or at least it seemed that way to A.D., until Wesley swung his feet up on the sofa and fell into a dreamless sleep.

WESLEY slept into the middle of the next day and woke to the sound of the plane taking off across the bay. He lay for a long time without moving, watching patches of sunlight thick with dust slice into the room. Outside a board banged and the wind rose and whistled around the house before howling off toward the southwest. He remembered that wind. It was an autumn wind and it would blow for weeks until the ice came in. It would be a time of preparation. The boats would be hauled and the houses banked and the last of the wood cut. The light would grow dim and sullen and when the snow and ice came there would be nothing to do at all. Not even wait. Perhaps not even remember. He stood up. Someone must have removed his clothes and it was cold enough so that he hurried to dress. Then he went into the kitchen.

Long was frying mackerel and potatoes. Coffee was on and the room was warm from the stove. Wesley poured himself a cup of coffee and sat down.

"I'll be drifting off," Long said. "Got my own shack down by the shore and it'll do."

"There's enough room here for both of us," Wesley said.

"Not for this child there ain't. The whole panorama won't never be the same since you landed, Wesley Hardin. Course, that ain't true, either. I never seen a day that wasn't the same on Slab Island. Even yesterday. That was the same. And tomorrow won't be no different. Now me, I figure to make it through the spring thaw, enough to put out a trap line."

"I'll partner with you," Wesley offered.

Long dropped the mackerel and potatoes onto a plate and shook his head. "I always set my own traps. Sell my own pelts. Chew my own 'baca. Never partnered and never will. Not on the sea. Not on the land. Otherwise what would be the sense? But I'll plug you enough meat to last the freeze up."

"I can plug my own meat," Wesley said.

"You got to put it in the pan," Long said.

"I can manage that, too."

Long nodded, his mouth full of food. After he had finished eating, he slung a burlap sack over his shoulder with all his worldly goods inside and went out the door without a word.

Wesley sat in the kitchen until the fire in the stove went out. Then he went outside.

There were no boats out and dark clouds were sliding across the sun. On the other side of town someone was cutting wood with a chain saw and beneath him by the shore a family of Inuit were building a fish rack. He was standing in his socks, wearing only his pants and a thin cotton shirt, and the wind felt raw, almost painful. Beyond the harbor, long dirty swells were rolling in toward the breakwater. No planes would land this day, or the day after, and soon the ice would form and it would be weeks before a plane would come in.

He walked around the house and then went back inside and it was only after he had built a fire again and was sitting at the kitchen table waiting for the kettle to boil that Wesley realized he was for the moment, and perhaps even finally, alone.

This project was coordinated by Lisa Janssen,
with assistance from Laura Pearson.

The text of this book was assembled in Adobe InDesign CS5
by Dan Osborn. It was typeset and proofread in Chicago, Illinois,
and then printed and bound by Bang Printing in Brainerd, Minnesota.

The text face used in this book is Adobe Caslon Pro, designed by
Carol Twombly, based on original Caslon specimen pages printed
by William Caslon between the years 1734 and 1770.

The paper is 55# Heritage Tradebook Cream.
It is of archival quality, acid-free, and is certified
by the Sustainable Forest Initiative.

Rudolph Wurlitzer
is the author of five novels:
Nog, *Flats*, *Quake*, *Slow Fade*, and most
recently, *The Drop Edge of Yonder*.

He is equally well-known as a
screenwriter, responsible for the scripts
for *Two-Lane Blacktop*, *Glen and Randa*,
Pat Garrett and Billy the Kid, *Walker*,
and *Candy Mountain*.

He is also the author of
Hard Travel to Sacred Places,
a travel diary of East Asia.

Presently, he and his wife, photographer
Lynn Davis, split their time between Hudson,
New York, and Cape Breton, Nova Scotia.